HOPE ENDURES

BOOK TWO IN THE SERIES OF HOPE

EMILY STALDER JOHNSON

CLAY BRIDGES
P R E S S

Hope Endures
Book Two in the Series of Hope
Fifth Edition

Published by Clay Bridges in Houston, TX
www.ClayBridgesPress.com

Scripture quotations are taken from the King James Version (KJV): King James Version, public domain.

ISBN: 978-1-953300-14-0
eISBN: 978-1-953300-15-7

Special Sales: Clay Bridges titles are available in wholesale quantity. Please visit www.claybridgesbulk.com to order 10 or more copies at a retail discount. Custom imprinting or excerpting can also be done to fit special needs. Contact Clay Bridges at Info@ClayBridgesPress.com.

TABLE OF CONTENTS

DEDICATION

I dedicate this book to my late grandmother Dona Rae Stalder, whom I loved dearly. I will always remember her love of books and her love for and devotion to her family.

Grandma, I will always rejoice in the knowledge that I will someday be reunited with you. I hope that somehow you know just how much I miss you and how important you have always been to me.

Thank you for encouraging me to read as a child and beyond, and for being so supportive of my writing. I won't forget how you shared in my joy of becoming an author. I hope I've made you proud. I have always looked up to you. Rest in peace, my dear Grandma Stalder.

Love,
Miss Em

I also want to dedicate this book to my dearest sister in Christ, Cassie Hendrickson—my best friend since high school—and her loving mother, Sandra "Sam" Hendrickson, best known as Mom to me. I love you both, and I deeply appreciate you more than words could ever express. I thank God for our friendship that quickly evolved into being family. I am grateful for your support, your help, your love, and all the fun we've had.

And I can't forget my "other dad." I want to dedicate this book to my late adoptive father, Thomas Hendrickson, who was an incredible man and a great daddy who Cassie, Mom, and I lost too soon. Auntie Em loves you and misses you so much, Daddy.

All my love in the world I give to this loving, supportive family who accepted me as one of their own and impacted my life for the better.

CHAPTER ONE

Brushing the sweat from his brow, Andrew Caldwell exhaled deeply. Then, with great effort, he hefted his horse's saddle onto the gelding's sturdy back. Faithful old Midnight turned his ebony head, glancing sideways at his gentle owner. He nickered softly, his expression gentle and curious. Perhaps he was curious about where they might go today for their ride. It was almost as though he was also making certain that Andy was alright.

"I'm doing fine, old buddy," Andy reassured the aging horse.

Andy felt as though he was aging rapidly. He was only 42 years old, nearing 43, but he easily could have been mistaken for a man more up in years. Still, he remained thankful that God had allowed him to live this long. He was truly thankful that the Lord had enriched his life in an unexplained, fulfilling, and wondrous way. These last few, blessed years had been especially rewarding and renewing to his soul.

His heart warmed as a contented smile pulled at his lips, revealing a couple of deeply etched lines at the corners of his dark brown eyes and a few more near his mouth on either side. Yes, all things considering, Andy's life had been good. Life had also been good for his son, Dublin—the boy who was now almost a man.

He's a good young man, Andy thought. *I couldn't be any prouder of him if I tried.*

Andy took pride in Dublin's progress, his growth, and particularly the healing he'd experienced. In spite of what the boy had been through, he had grown abundantly in countless areas of his life. And he'd been granted a merciful and God-led opportunity for a healing experience. The teenager seemed content with his life, to be living it alongside his papa, just the two of them on their horse farm. That pleased Andy beyond measure.

As dusk drew near, Andy led his horse out of the barn that housed all 10 of his magnificent Arabians and his six Quarter Horses, Midnight included.

The black horse trod slowly behind Andy. But Midnight was still as sure-footed and reliable a mount as he'd always been. While he wasn't as fleet as he'd been as a younger horse, he still held a certain liveliness about him.

Midnight's loyalty and temperament were, in Andy's opinion, exceedingly admirable. The gelding, around 20 years old now, was certainly an affectionate, mild-tempered creature whom Andy had always been able to trust as his everyday riding horse. Ever since the day Andy—a much younger man then—had bought him, Midnight had been ready to work.

When Andy first brought him home, Midnight was no more than an untamed four-year-old. Andy trained Midnight himself, discovering with satisfaction that the horse soon proved to be a reliable mount and a delightful companion.

It was May 1881 and an altogether sunny, warm, breezy Sunday evening. The weather had been consistently warm for the past two weeks. It was refreshing, for the previous month had been unpredictable, complete with randomly chilly bites here and there, sometimes lasting several days in a row. The cold made one question whether it would actually get warm in the spring before soon transforming into the more predictably hot, humid season of summer.

Andy placed his left foot into the stirrup on Midnight's near side before swinging into the impeccable Western saddle. After Andy settled properly into his seat, horse and rider set off. Midnight trotted through the vast woodlands that belonged to Andy, the land that had been willed to him after his parents' deaths. But that was a long, long time ago. No sense growing upset now.

Andy decided to focus on the beautiful shades of vibrant greens and other colors that were all around him—the trees, the bushes, the mossy rocks, and the varieties of wildflowers. They were as though an artist's perfectly skilled brush strokes had painted them—bright, diverse, beautiful shades of complementary violets, pinks, blues, reds, and yellows abundantly visible to the eye.

A wide assortment of birds sang cheerfully, making a pleasant environment for Andy's laid-back ride. Then he caught sight of a magnificent, red-tailed hawk suddenly taking flight from its perch, a lofty branch on a tall locust tree. Andy smiled at God's beautiful creation—the hawk, the other birds, the breathtaking landscape. All the intermingling sounds of wildlife were marvelous, even soul-soothing to him.

Then there were the cunning red and gray fox squirrels scampering up and down the trees here and there, chattering incessantly. There were soft, rustling sounds and the creaking of the swaying tree branches from the light breeze, pulling and pushing them, all adding to the pleasantness of the wondrous nature around him.

It was nearing 6:00 in the evening, but the sun had not yet begun to set. Andy still had time for this calming ride before dusk would set in. Andy's thoughts returned once again to his only son, Dublin, his wonderful son he'd spontaneously adopted one October day back in 1878. Dublin, then 14, had been at the mercy of his biological father's drunken fury. Andy had quickly put an end to the beating. He recalled his own fury that the boy was being treated so badly. Undeserving, indeed, young Dublin had faced a senseless whipping at the hands of Anthony Pearson, a troubled, mean-spirited man, certainly a man unworthy to be called the boy's father.

Anthony had felt compelled to whip Dublin after the boy had ridden off on one of Anthony's prized horses in a desperate attempt to escape the horrific abuse he'd been enduring since his mother had died. Andy had managed to chase off the boy's father, and then his heart began to open up, welcoming Dublin into it as his very own son. Love, protectiveness, and a strong, burning desire to provide for all Dublin's needs immediately kindled warmly within Andy's soul.

Although Andy was no more than a well-meaning stranger, Dublin willingly, trustingly, and desperately went home with him. The boy rapidly grew rather affectionate toward Andy. He soon loved him as the father he'd always prayed for, seemingly in vain. Dublin's heart began to heal right away. He'd finally been granted a loving father, although he still lacked the belief that God above loved him. No matter how much Andy tried to convince him of the Lord's love for him, Dublin couldn't accept it.

That void in Dublin's heart consumed him, leaving him without the only love that can ever truly satisfy a person. Regardless of his understandable doubts of God's presence in his life, Dublin grew increasingly curious about whether there was a God who intended good for him. But his warring emotions, his fears, his pain, and his past prevented him from accepting that he could receive new life—a new, hopeful life through God's unfailing love—by accepting and therefore knowing Jesus.

The day came that Anthony Pearson somehow fatefully crossed their paths once again. Dublin's world was shaken and shattered within seemingly a moment's time. Dublin, a helpless bystander, felt unspeakable despair when Anthony, filled with hate and fury, succumbed to a gunshot wound that Andy's barn manager fired just in time trying to save Dublin from being shot in the head by the crazed man.

Overwhelmed by confusion and fear, Dublin lost all hope of his situation ever improving. He felt further away from God than ever before, which grieved him deeply. Guilt-ridden that Andy had been shot trying to protect him, he added this encounter to the growing list inside his heart of all his grave failures with God.

It didn't help that Anthony had died begging only for Dublin's forgiveness, that he'd crossed into eternity without expressing any love for his son. Dublin had numbly taken Andy's gun, holding it to his temple, intending to end his life.

But praise God! Andy had emptied the weapon of all its bullets before Dublin's desperate attempt to end his pain. Upon realizing the gun was empty, Dublin sank to his knees, crying out to God in his heart as he surrendered all he had and who he was to the Lord.

Years of pain, disappointment, utter heartache, and tears were washed away. New waves of hope, love, unexplained joy, relief, and peace came over him and soon eradicated all the old, burdensome emotions that had eaten away at him. The bitterness and resentment toward God and his thoughts of hatred and bitter vengeance toward Anthony were removed in an instant. Those dark and heavy feelings he thought had belonged to him were miraculously lifted.

Andy later recalled how Dublin had tearfully shared his salvation with him, every detail of it, shortly after he was baptized in the spring of 1879. Clearly, the boy was changed, and for the better. He was on a path of life to the fullest with the possibility of limitless spiritual growth. And he was at the beginning of a long and satisfying path, forever filled with many good and promising things for him.

No matter the imminent future struggles, pain, and temptation, no matter what hardships life would bring his way, he'd emerge as the victor because of what Jesus had done, was doing, and would continue to do for him.

Andy had suffered severe injuries at the hands of Anthony Pearson. When he awakened from the trauma of his injuries, he joyfully welcomed Dublin's declaration of his recent salvation. Determined to help Dublin remain strong through any adversity that might threaten his progress and peace-filled life, Andy took on the role of Dublin's mentor as well as his father.

Andy's mind now shifted to the present. He knew his 17-year-old son was out riding his own horse, his Paint mare, Marguerite. Dublin often went out for long rides by himself, spending time in prayer. Andy was happy to allow him to go for as long as he wished. The teenager, he knew, needed this time to himself to bond with his Heavenly Father and continue healing from a past that still sometimes haunted him.

When Andy had saddled up Midnight, Dublin had already been gone for three hours or so. While he wasn't particularly worried for his son, his absence was noticeable around the farm. Since it was Sunday, Andy's employees and his barn supervisor weren't there. Andy missed having someone to talk to.

So here he was, on his own expedition, hoping to cross paths with his son. He knew the youth would not mind if the two of them happened to meet up. Andy slowed Midnight down to a walk as they went deeper into the woods. He allowed his horse to move about at a more relaxed pace. A thought suddenly crossed Andy's mind.

Why, I'll just about bet Dublin's at the river, sitting under the willow tree. I suppose I'll ride out that way to see him.

Smiling, Andy reined Midnight toward the Teays River. But once they arrived, he saw that Dublin wasn't there. He and Marguerite were definitely nowhere in sight. Frowning, Andy now felt a rising concern for his son begin to painfully radiate within his chest. A silent prayer was on his lips. Shaking his head, he tried to reason with himself that the teen was just out riding still, just somewhere else.

This isn't a catastrophe. Dublin is likely just fine.

But then why did he feel this uneasy?

CHAPTER TWO

Andy rode his horse throughout all the woods on his property, scanning for any sight of his son. Despite his thorough, frantic efforts, the boy was nowhere to be found.

Andy's concern for Dublin was becoming more and more palpable. What bothered him the most was that he knew something was wrong, but he didn't know what exactly was wrong or where in the world Dublin could be. The hairs at the back of Andy's neck stood on end. He attempted to call out Dublin's name, but his voice caught in his throat. Nothing but a quiet, strangled cry escaped his lips.

Twice more he tried to call for his son, but his voice remained as though it were paralyzed. So he rode all the more frantically, searching around every boulder and in every crevice, large shade tree, and cave—anywhere Dublin could be lying hurt or ill.

Perhaps he's unconscious. Oh, Lord, what do I do? Help me, Father, so I can help him.

Andy couldn't shake the awful feeling that something was terribly wrong. His instincts had proven to be mostly accurate in times past. And that frightened him.

Lord God, please keep my son safe in Your hands until I can find him. If something really is wrong, please shield him from further danger, and give him Your protection. Thank You, and it's in Jesus's name I pray. Amen.

Andy trekked farther across his land, backtracking until he finally came across Marguerite standing quietly in an area he'd somehow overlooked during his search. She was ground-hitched by a grassy knoll and currently without a rider.

"Marguerite, girl. Where is our Dublin?" Andy asked the grazing horse despairingly. The bay-and-white Paint lifted her head, leveling her piercing, sky-blue eyes at Andy's own desperate gaze.

Even though Andy knew the mare couldn't offer a reply, inside he hoped she would somehow help him find his son. Stunned, Andy stared open-mouthed as the Paint Quarter Horse tossed her head with a snort. Then she disregarded her ground-hitch command that had been issued to her at some point.

Amazed even further, Andy watched as the mare began to wander northwest toward an especially thickly wooded area of the property. Realizing that Andy and Midnight weren't trailing after her, she turned her head and looked back at Andy, almost beckoning him to follow her.

All right, well, maybe she cannot offer a verbal reply, but she is clearly leading me to something. Perhaps to my boy. Please, Father God, let Dublin be alright. I . . . I can't bear it if . . . Please, Lord. Please.

What disconcerted Andy the most was the near silence of the woods rather than the occasional musical strains of various songbirds. He couldn't hear any sounds that Dublin might be making. If he was injured, he was completely silent.

Andy was terrified. He wished he could at least hear his son calling for him or hear him moaning. Something. Anything. Some audible sound that would assure him that Dublin was . . . was still . . .

Alive.

Don't be silly. Don't even think like that. Just follow his horse and get to him, along with a level head, and then—help him!

Shortly thereafter, Marguerite halted. Andy frantically scanned the surroundings for his missing, potentially injured son. His chocolate-brown eyes then settled on a small rock formation, cave-like in structure but hollowed out only a few feet deep inside. Next to the mouth of the tiny cave lay Dublin Caldwell, awkwardly crumpled on the ground. He was unconscious. Blood stained his shirt on his left side, and his shirt was ripped where it was bloody. It also appeared that his head was resting against a rock. His right cheek was bleeding, too, on the side where he lay.

No!

Andy, forgetting any prior feelings of weariness or weakness, sprang into action. Dismounting, he immediately rushed to his unconscious son's side. The lean teenager was a bit slight for his age compared to some of the other boys in the London, Ohio, area. He looked even smaller now in his current, vulnerable position.

Dismayed, Andy quickly surmised that Dublin had been a victim of a shooting. Suddenly, he recalled hearing a gun fired earlier in the day—perhaps a mere 45 minutes into Dublin's ride.

Andy hadn't thought much of it since men frequently hunted in the woods near his property. Andy had given a couple of fellows who lived close to his farm permission to hunt on his land. He hadn't heard anything else that might indicate it was something other than a shot fired at wild game. The deer were abundant in this area, so he'd naturally but unfortunately assumed someone had been out and about on the hunt for wild game.

Deeply disturbed, worried, and perplexed by what had happened and how, Andy knelt next to his son. "Dublin. Son. Can you hear me? It's your papa. Will you open your eyes?"

He looked at the boy's wounds, and although his clothing, some of his hair, and the affected skin were stained with blood, it appeared that the bleeding had stopped long before his arrival to the scene. Andy could see that the bullet, which seemed to have grazed Dublin's ribs, had probably knocked him to the ground. Consequently, he must have hit his head on the rock where his head currently rested.

Andy walked over to Midnight and took a large canteen of water from one of the gelding's saddlebags. Then he jogged back to where Dublin lay and opened the canteen. He slowly poured the cool water against Dublin's bloody brow, hair, and parts of his right cheek that weren't pressed against the rock.

Almost immediately and to Andy's everlasting relief, Dublin's dark blue eyes opened at once. He lifted his battered head, jolted by the shock of cold water that flowed against his face. Letting out a strangled cry, he was soon reacquainted with the pain.

"Papa!" Dublin cried out weakly. He moved to rise into a sitting position but stopped short, grimacing at the pain from his wound.

"Dublin, my son. Dear Lord, what happened? Are you alright? I need to get you to Jacob's office right away," Andy said all at once as Dublin was managing to sit up.

Dublin looked at his papa through pain-dimmed eyes. He swayed a little, was ultimately able to steady himself, but then realized he was beginning to collapse again. He tentatively shook his head, trying to clear his mind and focus better. Sharp pains stabbed at him all over the right side of his head.

But he was overcome with relief that his beloved papa was there with him, that he'd somehow known exactly where to find him and had come to his aid. Dublin cleared his throat, his deep voice sounding momentarily.

"Papa, ouch! No, I mean, I'm alright. I was just, uh, out riding. The last thing I can recall was seeing a tall, big man far off in the distance riding a dark-colored, draft-type horse. He stopped, and then he aimed his rifle at me."

Dublin paused for a few moments and then continued. "As I started to flee, the bullet hit me and knocked me off Marguerite. I must have fallen and hit my head pretty badly because I don't remember anything after that—not until I woke up and you were here."

He sounded to Andy to be both greatly relieved and vastly perturbed, and understandably so. Andy frowned, also greatly bothered. He wasn't sure who the unknown man atop a draft horse could have been. But what he *did* know was that he needed to get his son to the doctor and report this information to the town sheriff, Daniel Walters.

Thank You, God, that my son wasn't more seriously injured.

Andy gently hugged his son with one arm as a small, lone tear escaped his left eye, mainly from relief. His heart broke, though, that his son had been targeted, knowing full well he could have been killed. His heart broke that Dublin was enduring even more pain in his young life. The thoughts both enraged him and caused him to feel such sorrow.

Anyone who knew Dublin knew he was a kind soul who'd never harm a fly. Nor would he do anything to ever purposefully invoke rage in another human being. His past unpleasant experiences with his late biological father and with a haughty, intolerant former teacher were not because of the boy's shortcomings.

That teacher was Mr. Carter Fallon. Well, he'd definitely harbored a grudge against Andy Caldwell and subsequently against Dublin. It all began on Dublin's first day at his new school. Dublin feared the hot-tempered school teacher, for the man was about to punish him with his hickory switch over something ridiculous—adopting Andy's last name as his own.

For some reason, Dublin's resolute declaration of his new surname had resulted in Mr. Fallon's unforeseeable rage. Frightened but determined not to be beaten by a man who didn't know the half of his past, Dublin had frantically wriggled free of Fallon's grasp. Then he fled on his horse, heading safely toward Andy's horse farm—toward *his* new home.

Once he made it there, he relayed his experiences with the unreasonable teacher to his new father. Now, at this unwanted recollection, Andy's anger boiled up in his chest. He pushed away the memories of that encounter. But as he remembered Carter Fallon's horse, he knew it wasn't any sort of draft horse.

No. It couldn't have been him.

Fallon currently—remarkably—was a reliable handyman around town. He now rode a rather distinct white-and-gray Appaloosa mare. Dotted all over her were large, white splashes and beautiful, dark gray spots of varying sizes, all forming to make a pretty pattern. Her mane and tail were dark gray, both very sparse.

Appaloosas were bred like that to prevent entanglement in brush and in the general wilderness and prevent their hair from being in the Native

Americans' way during combat. It would have been a very unique horse for Dublin to see and describe had his assailant been Fallon. But Dublin hadn't described a horse like that. Not even close.

Not that Andy truly believed his old adversary would ever resort to firing a rifle at Dublin, but it made no sense that a stranger—on Andy's own land, no less—would shoot the nearly grown young man without provocation. Undeniably, it was a great mystery that had Andy rattled.

Dublin was experiencing pain—pain that Andy could help try to lessen for him if he could just get Dublin up onto Marguerite and take him over to his best friend's medical practice.

Jacob will know exactly what to do, Andy thought.

"Here, Dublin—let me pour some water on your side to wash away some of the blood. It'll cool your wound, too."

Seeing Dublin nod, Andy promptly carried out his suggestion. The water was refreshing against Dublin's torn skin. He sighed as it flowed over the wound, washing away the blood and relieving some of the pain. Andy then inspected the wound more closely now that he could actually see it and its depth. Thank God, the bullet wound wasn't deep. Not at all.

But Dublin's pale skin, marked with both the injury and old scars from Dublin's past, was very red and irritated. Still to this day, Andy was relieved that Anthony Pearson was dead, mainly for Dublin's safety. Even so, it was apparent that the boy was still unsafe around here.

With a prayer in his heart, Andy wordlessly assisted Dublin to his feet. The boy precariously made his way slowly to his chivalrous mare who'd valiantly led his papa over to where he'd lain, wounded and alone. Dublin swung himself up onto Marguerite's saddle, grunting from his effort and the awful discomfort. He closed his eyes, reins in hand, and took a few slow, deep breaths.

Watching through sapphire eyes as Andy climbed aboard his own loyal mount, Dublin remembered fondly that it was Midnight who'd carried Andy to his rescue. He was the horse who would then carry the two of them safely to Andy's home and far away from danger. Andy's home had quickly become Dublin's home and remained his home to this day.

They directed their horses through the woods and headed out to the dirt road that would lead them away from Andy's property and to the town of London, Ohio. Neither of them said anything. Both were too preoccupied saying silent prayers of thanksgiving to God. The Lord had clearly looked out for Dublin once again, just like He always had.

God had ensured Andy that he would find Dublin, this time using Marguerite to lead the way. It simply wouldn't have worked any other way. The fact that Dublin's horse had done what she had was in itself a remarkable miracle.

Praise God!

Wearily, they made their way to Dr. Nicholas's medical practice. Andy helped Dublin as he awkwardly stumbled toward the building, supporting him so he wouldn't fall.

Jacob Nicholas wasn't usually at his practice on Sundays. But Andy and Dublin had already tried to meet up with him at his home and found he wasn't there. Sure enough, his horse, Lady, was tethered outside the medical building, surrounded by two troughs that were filled with food and water. Jacob's trusty mare was also sheltered by a wooden lean-to. She was comfortable on most days while she was tethered in that area during her master's working hours. The pretty horse would remain there patiently while her master faithfully and compassionately worked on the ill and the injured of London, Ohio, throughout the week, and on emergency calls.

Jacob was inside, alone, working on paperwork at his desk. Thankfully, he had no patients in the beds needing care overnight. It was a good thing for sure since he had no assistance from either of his nurses. Neither Ida nor Grace was required to work on Sundays. For Sundays, along with most Saturdays, were their days off. In certain circumstances, though, when Jacob needed their help, he would send for them, but that was a rarity.

Jacob looked up from his papers in his office when he heard footsteps on the hard wooden floor in his foyer. Rushing from his seat in his private office, he quickly came face-to-face with his best friend and his son.

Aside from being close friends and basically family, these two were, unfortunately, some of his most frequent patients for one reason or another. And here was Dublin, barely able to remain upright.

"Andy! Dublin! What's happened?" Jacob cried.

He was startled by the sight of Dublin's bruised and bloody face, as well as his ripped shirt that exposed an irritated, red wound across his ribs. Why, it looked to him like the 17-year-old had been shot.

CHAPTER THREE

"Oh, Jake, we don't know," Andy responded, melancholy and worry evident in his baritone voice. "Someone took a shot at him earlier today."

Sighing, Jacob guided them into the room closest to them. He helped Andy sit Dublin on a cot. Dublin, still shaken and in pain, found himself unable to say anything or answer any questions the doctor asked. Though he was grateful that God had saved him again, this time from a far worse fate—he was also weary. It was as though all the energy in his body drained from his being the moment he settled down on the cot.

He was vaguely aware of Dr. Nicholas unbuttoning his ruined shirt and then gently pulling it from his torso. And it was as though he was there but simultaneously far away elsewhere. He was now acutely aware that his scars were exposed, not that Andy and Dr. Nicholas hadn't seen them before. Even so, he did not care for people to look upon them. They still caused him to feel self-conscious and shameful. They would forever bear witness of the pain—all the violence he'd endured from times past—left behind from recurrent attacks by a man who'd deemed him defective, unlovable, and unworthy of anything good.

Dublin wished he could crawl under the blankets on the cot he sat upon. Instead, he remained compliant to the doctor's examination and the thorough cleaning of his side and head wounds. Dr. Nicholas was gentle and compassionate throughout the whole process. While he worked, he spoke with Andy regarding Dublin's predicament. His tone was somber.

Dublin was thankful that he couldn't feel any additional pain while the kindly doctor tended to his injuries. Once the doctor finished up his work, Dublin's wounds felt better. He now had a small, clean bandage over the gash on his head and a larger one covering the wound on his side.

"Dublin, Andy—you both should know that Dublin is going to be just fine," the doctor reported. "His wounds are not deep, and there isn't any sign of infection or any other complications from what I can see. They will heal perfectly; just give it some time. You two may go home now—and Andy, you need to speak with Sheriff Walters come tomorrow morning. Alert him about what happened today. I'll be praying that this man won't cause any more trouble for Dublin and you, or anyone else in this town, for that matter. Go home and get some rest. It's nearing upon 8:00 now, and you two have endured an awfully eventful and traumatic day." The doctor smiled compassionately at his friends.

"Thank you, Jake," Andy said simply. His heart was glad that all would be well with Dublin.

"You are most welcome. Now, please, try to stay away from any more danger, both of you. Please!"

Andy nodded, a solemn expression on his handsome face. Then he paid Jacob for his services to his son. The doctor attempted to refuse payment, but with some effort, Andy convinced his friend that he ought not attend to him and Dublin without accepting payments for his time, effort, and the use of his medical supplies. Jacob reluctantly took the money, but he smiled graciously. Giving Andy a hearty pat on the back, he then reached out and gently touched Dublin's shoulder.

Dublin shook the doctor's hand. "Thank you, Dr. Nicholas."

"Of course, Dublin. You know I'd go to the ends of the earth to help you and your papa stay well, son. God bless the both of you, and have a safe ride home."

Father and son nodded as they turned to walk out the door. They were greeted by a much cooler breeze out now than had blown about all day. It was beginning to grow dusky, but they would make it home before nightfall.

But then Andy remembered with a start that all his horses were still out to pasture. Although it was 6:00 in the evening when Andy set out to find Dublin, he left his horses in the field with the intention of bringing them all inside once he and Dublin returned to the horse farm together. He certainly hadn't planned on Dublin's being injured and then having to make a trip into town.

They made it home safe and sound. Sighing wearily, Andy dismounted Midnight and led him into the barn after undoing the latch across the double doors. Dublin followed suit, and they put up their horses for the night after removing their tack.

Dublin was exhausted, too. But he insisted on taking care of his own horse because, while he was tired and in pain, he could clearly see that his father looked as haggard and troubled as he felt, perhaps even more. Andy didn't refuse. He knew if Dublin ever offered or insisted to do work, despite an injury or illness, he did so in the knowledge that he'd be able to complete the task.

Andy was tempted to leave his horses out in the pasture overnight but immediately thought better of that notion. They were his livelihood, the way he paid his bills. What if the man who'd shot his precious son returned to steal or harm his horses? While his son was more important to him, of course, they still had to eat. He shook his head and sighed.

After Dublin finished with his horse, he told Dublin that he could retire to bed if he wished while he rounded up all the other horses. Dublin sighed, feeling torn. He wanted to assist his father, but he predicted that he wouldn't be able to keep up for long enough to be helpful. Reluctantly, he chose to call it an evening. Wordlessly hugging his papa, he turned toward the farmhouse and went inside.

Dublin realized suddenly that he hadn't had anything to eat since lunchtime. However, he decided he was simply too tired to try to cook something, despite the hunger pangs. Andy wasn't in any shape to do anything more, so Dublin wasn't about to ask him to make him something.

Tired and defeated, Dublin slowly trod up the staircase, making his way to his bedroom. Kicking off his boots and then removing his shirt, he crawled into his comfortable bed shortly after he opened his bedroom window. Instantly, the cool breeze swirled inside his room comfortingly.

It helped calm him enough to say his nighttime prayers before falling asleep. He dreamed of many fun, lighthearted times he'd spent in contentment with Andy Caldwell, his beloved father for around three years—Andy, his papa who'd replaced Anthony Pearson in a most welcoming and fulfilling manner.

Sometime after Dublin was fast asleep, Andy finally completed his duties on his own and turned in for the night. He fell almost immediately into a hard sleep. About that time, Dublin's dreams suddenly altered into a frightening nightmare. He whimpered softly in his sleep as a bad memory from long ago painfully resurfaced. Dublin was just a slight 10-year-old, overcome with fear. He stood, fairly shaking in his tight-fitting shoes, cowering before Anthony Pearson who shouted at him without mercy. His small shoulders hunched as the weight of his father's harsh words crushed his spirits.

Young Dublin stood in the round cattle barn that remained on their property even though it was essentially unused for anything other than storage. Standing next to it was Anthony's horse barn, and to the west of that barn was the pasture where he kept his prized Thoroughbreds. Anthony loved those stunning horses more than his young, impressionable boy. Dublin had learned this already, this sad fact that he was of significantly less worth than the graceful, spirited animals.

Even though Dublin was Anthony's only son and he favored his father in appearance, he simply wasn't wanted. Already accustomed to being beaten with his father's belt or other objects handy for Anthony to grab in a flash of anger, Dublin feared but expected the treatment that was frequently handed down to him. And somehow he knew in the pit of his stomach that it was about to happen again. Just like always, and it was going to begin soon. He began to feel sick to his stomach.

He wasn't really all too surprised when Anthony hollered at him to remove his shirt—the filthy, ragged, too small shirt. Dublin, shaking in fear at the impending punishment, immediately obeyed without protest if but to keep from angering his father even further. He thought with minimal hope that if he quickly complied, perhaps his punishment might be less severe. He held on to that hope for the time being.

Anthony growled, placing his heavy hand on Dublin's bare shoulder, shoving the almost emaciated, altogether frightened 10-year-old up against the southern wall of the barn. Dublin's face was pressed against the wooden planks of the wall. He put his hands against the boards for support and closed his eyes as his heart raced furiously. But something was alarmingly different this time.

The eerie whistle of the whip as it sliced crisply through the air suddenly reached his ears before the loud, unnerving crack could be heard as it struck his back. Paralyzed by the fear, Dublin simply cried out in pain from the great force of the blow, frightened from the terrifying sounds. He found he couldn't even try to move to escape since the pain consumed him entirely. And he didn't want to find out what his father would do to him when he caught him. Unrelentingly, the pain increased intolerably as the beating continued. Fearfully, Dublin screamed every time he was struck until his throat felt nearly as raw and aflame as his back.

Once he finally sank weakly to his knees, hopelessly defeated, he cried as his father finally yielded, only to resume his shouting at the bleeding, panic-stricken boy.

"I hate you, Dublin James Pearson! You are a sorry excuse for a son. You couldn't be any more of a disappointment than you are, and I swear to God that I won't hesitate to whip you again like this the next time you cross me, young man. Do you hear me?"

Anthony paused. "Do you hear me?" he roared, leaning in close, right next to his son's ear.

Crying out in fear and still sobbing shamefully, Dublin flinched. He managed to offer a submissive reply. "Yes, sir. I...I hear you, Father."

His voice was notably timid and soft in pitch. But inside, despite his fearfulness and pain, he spoke a silent but fierce mantra within his heart. *I hate you, too. I wish you would die!* Yet even though that was his unspoken truth, he somehow still desperately craved his father's love. Somehow, amid the hatred for his father, he simultaneously felt some love for him, even after all he'd done. Tears coursed furiously down his cheeks as his heart broke in sadness and shame. But soon he was angry.

Lost in a sea of hopelessness and utter confusion, he remained in the barn as his father stalked off, leaving him all alone, bleeding and in pain. What seemed strange to him, though, was that the pain he felt most acutely was the pain inside his heart. It was nearly more than he could bear.

Dublin awoke from this dream suddenly, drenched in sweat. His heart raced at the vivid, unpleasant memory, a memory he wished would never surface again, along with all the other memories that occasionally plagued him.

The events of the previous day had been shocking and traumatic, but now it was early morning of the next day. Dublin realized he basically led a refreshingly hopeful, new life. His life was full of satisfying love, warmth, and healing now from both his papa and his God. He was very thankful for his home with Andy.

So, why wasn't I spared this memory, Lord?

Would he ever be healed of these memories that tormented him as he lay vulnerable and asleep? Even though the flashbacks were only sporadic, he did hope to one day be rid of them forever. If that were to happen, he believed he could experience what he thought to be true healing—to forget it all and focus only on the fact that his life was now significantly better, to remember that he had the most loving father. Andy was the best earthly father he could ever have hoped for.

Dublin wished to always bask blissfully in knowing he was blessed and to no longer dwell on his past. He certainly had a promising future now.

> *God, I want to focus on You now and on my life with my rightful father, Andy, and not think about Anthony any longer. Lord, You know I don't need to be reminded of all that pain and how I hated him so and even You, Lord, back then. I only want to live in the present and to live for You alone.*
>
> *Please, help me.*
>
> *I want to trust wholly in You, but it is so difficult when I dream of times past like this. Forgive me. I fail to see Your reasoning in allowing this. And help me. I want to obey You in all I do. I want to obey all Your callings and commands, whatever they may be.*
>
> *Whatever the cost.*

Forgive me for never being good enough to earn Your love, but I thank You for loving me so much anyway. No words can truly express how that makes me feel so loved by You on my good days, but if only I could feel Your love right now.

Amen.

Dublin lay there quietly, contemplating his dream, its purpose, and his silent prayer. It overwhelmed him. Several minutes later, he decided that if he was careless, he'd surely lie there until the sun rose for the day, mulling these things over with such an obsession so intense that he wouldn't be able to acquire any more rest. And he knew he would regret it.

He felt his resistance against resting drain from his body. He lay still, completely unmoving save for his controlled breathing—in and out. He chose to focus on his breathing with all his strength, attempting to think no more about all he'd processed mere moments ago. Instead, his thoughts resumed their screaming in his mind, just running and rerunning pointless, goalless laps in different directions. It nearly drove him mad.

Thoughts of doubt, confusion, and intense, deeply rooted hurt and injustice—all of it resurfaced, all the *whys* of how he was brought up that were still a mystery to him. He slid out of his bed, hoping the movement would distract his raging thoughts, that it would prevent tears from soon falling. Angrily, he shook his head.

He was angry with the prospect of crying just like an infant at the mature age of 17, no less. And he had to admit that he was also growing angry with God—all over again. Immediately, though, he grew remorseful. He considered all the ways God had saved him from far worse fates. God had always looked out for him. He'd *always* been there for him.

Forgive me, Lord.

But Lord, what is wrong with me that I seem to always be a target for violence?

God had done much for him. He'd taken such care of Dublin, ensuring him that he would always receive all he needed. "The Lord is nigh unto them that are of a broken heart; and saveth such as be of a contrite spirit.

Many are the afflictions of the righteous: but the LORD delivereth him out of them all." Dublin sighed with resignation but also in contentment as he recalled Psalm 34:18–19.

These were exactly the comforting and appropriate words he needed to remember at this precise moment. He felt like those holy words applied to his current and past situations, his great and numerous afflictions.

The scripture verses gave him a certain hope that God was, indeed, on his side and at his side, too, and that He would always be close by. The Lord was clearly looking out for him tirelessly, and although Dublin had been made right with Him, he still suffered. That may never change, he supposed. Even so, God would reliably come to his aid, delivering him from each and every storm.

He had faith in God. He wasn't alone anymore. The Lord would make certain that he would be alright and stronger, too. Dublin knew that God would never force him to fend for himself, using what little strength he possessed within himself. Rather, Dublin would rise victorious and complete with newfound strength and a refined character.

Learning priceless lessons of indisputable worth and wisdom after withstanding a storm would always be Dublin's goal. And God, through His silent but mysterious, perceivable voice, would comfort him during those trying situations. Through God's perfect, living Word, the Lord would continuously bring Dublin to new, revealing truths each time he obediently opened his Bible, even if he didn't really want to.

> *God is so merciful and filled with grace, He would never leave me. He won't.*

A great, comforting peace began to settle in Dublin's heart, replacing his troubled feelings. He strolled about his room. His heart began to calm, too. But he wondered if he'd ever see greater growth and wisdom than how far he'd already come. He'd already changed a lot since he was saved, but he still made so many mistakes despite the change. He felt stuck.

> *Am I really that teachable of a pupil? I'm so apt to doubt and quick to worry and stray.*

He did know that God would forgive him for all his shortcomings that were to come. God had already forgiven his failures and sins against Him and others. All Dublin had to do was ask, for God understood all that went on inside his painfully healing heart. The Lord had uniquely created Dublin for a reason. God knew everything about him.

That meant the world to Dublin. It was so marvelous to him to acknowledge this humbling truth. And the Lord, who had given Dublin His Spirit to teach him all truths and wisdom, why, that was nearly unbelievable. He knew he was on the right path. He just knew it.

Fleetingly, he wondered why God would put up with all his antics with such patience. But he quickly remembered that God is love, and that He loved him as a son. Andy was certainly patient with him, too—to a fault.

> *God is good,* Dublin thought. *He even sent His Son to die for all people, for all who would believe in Him and follow Him, all who give their lives to Him, all who surrender their hurting hearts to Him. It was all so He could have His beloved children with Him in heaven. There is no greater love than His. Hmm, I suppose it's as if He couldn't bear the thought of heaven without every person He's created, every person with their own individuality, gifts, and inherent worth.*

But Dublin knew that God left the decision up to His creation to accept the free gift of life, or not. Dublin's understanding was that not everyone would ultimately choose a relationship with God through Christ. For the Lord gave people free will to choose. God didn't want to force everyone to love Him. What kind of love would that really be? It would certainly not be a true form of genuine love at all.

Dublin felt like he'd been granted a new perspective and attitude. This realization humbled him and subsequently caused him to feel more loved by God than ever before. He quickly repented of the doubts he'd harbored regarding his unfailing Heavenly Father. He vowed to never grow angry with God again, for he never would have a valid reason, honestly. The Lord, who would always love him and keep all His promises, was undoubtedly with him right now.

Dublin returned to his bed, sinking down on it, this time on his belly, just like he used to as a kid. A long time ago, he quickly learned to do that to ease the pain from the beatings he frequently received on his back. Thankfully, that pain would never return. But lying on his stomach had become a habitual position, and he found it rather comfortable even today. Relaxing, he settled his face against his pillow and finally fell asleep.

CHAPTER FOUR

Andy awoke around 5:30 a.m. He discovered, sympathetically, that Dublin was still fast asleep and breathing heavily. The teenager was completely unresponsive as Andy tried waking him up for the day.

It was certainly a misfortune that the young man still suffered from nightmares. Even though his past could no longer physically harm him, it certainly continued to cause him significant emotional pain. The dreams would give Dublin no choice but to relive life as it once was with Dublin completely defenseless against them in their duration.

> *I know we are not in control exactly of what happens to us during our lives,* Andy prayed. *Only You, Heavenly Father, can change our circumstances. Please help Dublin and me to trust You, to put all our hopes in You, no one else. It is You who guides us among these storms that come our way. Lord, be with Dublin this morning and restore his troubled soul. Thank You for every single thing You do for us, Father. Amen.*

Compassion tugged at his heart throughout and following his prayer. But just as he spun around on his heels, ready to go downstairs to begin breakfast and hopefully finish it before making another attempt to wake his son, Dublin rose, too. The teenager was clearly in a good mood, bringing joy and relief to Andy.

Confusion suddenly collided with Andy's joyousness. Typically, Dublin would wake from his nightmares in a state of fearfulness or disarray. He usually didn't appear this genuinely happy and well.

> *It's amazing,* Andy thought, *the difference it makes in a person, having the love and hope of Jesus in his heart, especially during such trying times with all our seemingly senseless trials. Like what happened yesterday, whatever that was about. Have mercy upon us, Lord.*

"Oh, good morning, Papa," Dublin said brightly as soon as he crawled out of his bed. He began making his bed neatly. The smile on his face reassured Andy who was still overcome with a sense of surprise. He had a hopeful feeling for Dublin and his recovery, his day today, and the rest of his life.

It seemed nothing would ever break him. Andy's hope was that nothing could, that Dublin would always remain a strong man of God. He hoped Dublin would forever possess the innate strength he'd always been blessed with ever since Andy had unintentionally crossed paths with him.

> *Indeed, he has always been a strong boy. He had to be to survive, to make it to the point where I was able to intervene in his life.*

"Good morning, son. How is your side feeling this morning? I truly hope that you aren't in a great deal of pain." Andy felt significant aversion once again to his son's suffering.

Andy was trying hard to follow through with *his* part in his walk with Christ by placing all his trust in God and not questioning Him in anger and doubt. Andy knew he needed to submit fully to Him and live and rest peacefully in Him. Somewhere from within, he knew that God's will was perfect, for the Lord was totally in control of this and all the situations in their lives. It was their lives together as a close-knit family that made it complete with an irreplaceable and often unspoken—*unbreakable*—bond. It had become incredibly fulfilling for the two of them.

The second part of Matthew 28:20 crept comfortingly into Andy's heart almost instantly. "And, lo, I am with you always, even unto the end of the world. Amen."

Then Dublin's strong, ever-maturing voice broke Andy's quiet meditation as he stood tall in his son's doorway, a faraway look across his aging, clean-shaven face.

"No, not too much pain," Dublin stated. "Praise the Lord! Oh, and Papa? I realize it's still early, but let's go start breakfast. I'm hungry."

Andy chuckled at his son's energetic declaration. This was not nearly the first or the 50th time Dublin had roped him into starting breakfast or another meal while he had been lost in his thoughts, utterly distracted. It had always grated on his nerves to think how Dublin's asking Anthony for food might have been received back then. Andy was more than delighted to be redirected toward fixing a meal for his simply wonderful son—his precious son, his heart's reason for pressing on, the one he thanked God for every day and all day.

"Oh! Why certainly, my son! Come, let's go right away," Andy exclaimed, smiling.

Dublin's own radiant face perfectly reflected his papa's. Even though his face was bruised and scraped, he still appeared to be genuinely happy. In spite of the bruises and the scrapes, he *did* have an attractive, maturing face that at the same time was often boyish in appearance, such as when he'd grow excited about various things—food, riding, and horses in general.

God bless that boy! Bless the Lord, oh my soul!

Waves of love and admiration for his son moved over him, warming him. Andy placed his hand on Dublin's left shoulder before giving him a gentle hug. Then he ruffled his short, dark brown hair—just as he always had, nearly from day one.

Dublin's response was a low chuckle. He returned his father's hug with his left arm, squeezing his papa considerably harder than Andy had dared to squeeze him.

Andy exaggeratedly gasped, making loud, silly sounds as though he were in peril, but Dublin quickly caught on that his papa was being playful. His resounding laughter was soon infectious, a joyous sound to Andy's ears that started him laughing almost hysterically.

Soon, they both gasped out of true need since they had laughed so hard at Andy's coltish reaction to the youngster's antics for a solid few minutes.

"I am glad you seem to be feeling well, son," Andy said, shortly after he'd recovered.

Dublin sobered. He met his father's gaze. Though he was in a lighthearted mood, still, deep in the back of his mind, he felt like something was off from how it ought to be. Being shot by a stranger had been and still was terrifying.

Praise God, though. It could have been much worse.

Dublin had done nothing against the unknown man who'd tried to kill him. His thoughts turned toward the negative.

Life isn't fair.

Moments later, Dublin thought of a Bible verse. "Good and upright is the LORD: therefore will he teach sinners in the way. The meek will he guide in judgment: and the meek will he teach his way. All the paths of the LORD are mercy and truth" (Ps. 25:8–10). Dublin smiled at the recollection of the inspirational passage, which dependably invoked a little courage within his sensitive soul.

"Yes, Papa," Dublin murmured as he pondered the ancient words and all the ways God had made for him through his turbulent past. He thought, too, of the ways the Lord made life purposeful for him. God's love had brought such peace and fulfillment into his heart when it once was void of nearly all but turmoil, confusion, and pain. And all of that was in addition to the overwhelming loneliness and the painful emptiness he'd experienced daily. Oh, how he'd grown over the past few years!

They made their way downstairs and into the kitchen and put together a rather satisfying meal in very little time. Andy led them in prayer. Afterward, he and Dublin ate in silence, enjoying their meal, wondering about how the day might go. He still intended to speak with the sheriff in order to alert him to the unknown man who'd invaded Andy's property to hurt his son. It was all so gravely perturbing to him. Andy's distress over his son and the assailant compelled him to do something about the situation—but there wasn't much he *could* do. Not right now, anyway.

Wordlessly, Andy and Dublin washed their breakfast dishes. Andy scrubbed and rinsed the plates, the cutlery, and the cooking dishes with water freshly drawn from the springhouse. Dublin dried them before placing them in their designated spots in the various handcrafted cupboards. Completely content in the moment, the two of them headed outdoors, beginning their routine chores in the barn.

Feeding and watering all their horses, brushing them, picking their feet, and mucking out the stalls were all essential tasks that needing to be completed every day. Although it had become rather repetitive, Dublin never really minded the familiar work. It was satisfying physical labor, which made him feel productive, helpful, and needed. The work also kept him distracted from his often-wandering thoughts, and it wasn't especially burdensome.

In spite of his recent gunshot wound, the pain wasn't as severe as the pain he had dealt with each day living with Anthony in his home. Thank God this wasn't a serious injury. Miraculously, the bullet had only grazed his side. He still marveled at the situation. It could have been much, much worse. Still, his predicament was dire. He needed to be well aware of his surroundings in an attempt to try to maintain his safety around here—or anywhere.

I just need to keep my eyes to the Lord and keep on trusting in Him. And that's much easier said than done.

There had been many moments and periods of extended time when Dublin's faith in his loving and ever-constant Guide had faltered, where he'd slipped into doubt due to the circumstances in his life. Still, he somehow always found his way back to God. Or was it God who had always drawn him back? Either way, Dublin smiled as he reflected on how he'd been blessed since Andy had graciously adopted him, and even more so since he'd become a child of God.

The farm got finished quickly when Les Morrison, their barn supervisor, arrived for his morning shift along with the hired help, Frederick, Benjamin, Cameron, and Aaron. Andy spoke with Les before he went over his instructions for the day, instructions that Les would, in turn, relay to the other workers. Andy wanted Les and his employees to focus their attention on the two Arabian fillies that were almost four years old.

Quickly and privately, Andy also shared with Les the details of Dublin's assault from the previous day. Les strongly urged Andy to speak with the sheriff soon. He assured Andy that he and the employees would see to it that the work would be done just as Andy wanted it to be done.

Amazingly, the Arabian fillies were twins. Their mother, Amira, was an extravagant, vibrant, chestnut-colored mare. She'd delivered both foals at the time of their rare birth without complication. They were both incredibly strong and healthy, and healthy twin foals were not always common among horses. Andy hadn't been certain they would be in good health once he realized there were two on their way out of the smaller-sized Arabian broodmare.

The fillies were sired by, in Dublin's opinion, the most spectacular of Andy's Arabian stallions, Galal. He was uniquely colored with a smoky blue roan coat and a contrasting, unusual bright red mane and tail. Dublin had never seen a horse's mane and tail that color before, not with a blue-and-black-speckled coat pattern.

The foals' names were, in order of birth—though they were but minutes apart—Akilah and Kamaria. Right away, Akilah seemed to possess an innate cleverness, hence Andy's reasoning for her Arabian name. And Kamaria was given her name because of her coat, a lighter blue roan, milky with gray-white shades amid the faint blue tint. She had a dark gray mane and tail, just as the moon sometimes appears in the night sky. So Andy named her the Arabian name translated "the moon."

Unlike her sister, Akilah favored her dam. Like Amira, her coat was a rich, deep chestnut all over. Her mane and tail were interesting, with a beautiful combination of discernible dark and light red streaks throughout, including some sparse streaks of gray.

Andy and Dublin decided to assist Les and the workers for about 20 minutes, helping them first with the fillies. Shortly afterward, though, they saddled up their horses so they'd be able to soon ride onward and into London, Ohio. Dublin often rode the beautiful Paint Marguerite but today, he opted to ride his other Paint, Micah.

He loved the stallion dearly and enjoyed riding the impressive horse. He had helped Andy purchase the remarkable stallion with his own money, and Andy had allowed Dublin to care for him primarily and then decided the stallion should belong to Dublin in addition to the mare he'd given the boy. For that and many other reasons, Andy, in Dublin's honest opinion, was a very good man with a kindly heart. He hoped to grow to be as good a man as his papa was someday.

His horse Micah was a strikingly gorgeous black-and-white Paint. He was a Quarter Horse with piercing bright blue eyes. He was tall and especially well muscled. The stallion was truly beautiful to Dublin, who, from day one, had particularly appreciated Andy's Paints and their unique coat patterns that were quite unlike the coat colors on other horses.

Dublin was tightening the girth for the final time on Micah's saddle. Andy had already placed the bridle on the horse he'd chosen to ride today— Fareed, the beautiful sooty, dappled, buckskin Arabian stallion.

Because of his pain, Dublin moved about much more slowly than his papa. But his lagging behind was also understandable for another possible reason. The process of saddling a horse with an English saddle like Andy was saddling Fareed with could often go more quickly than completing all the required steps for its Western counterpart.

They mounted their stallions, setting off down the dirt driveway. They began riding the dusty road that would take them into London. It was already warming up comfortably now that it had been daylight for a while. The sun shone again, a brilliant beam in the sky. It was bright and clear out for another pleasant spring day. Fluffy, pure-white clouds amply decorated the light blue sky delightfully, and the radiant sun warmed Dublin deep within.

While the two of them rode at a leisurely pace, Andy suddenly realized he had hardly said a word to his son all morning long. He understood that he and Dublin were close, so they didn't necessarily always require much conversation, but it was more common for them to interact fairly frequently. He suddenly felt a pang of worry within his chest, wondering if Dublin wasn't actually doing alright.

"So, son, are you sure you're feeling well this morning? It's surely understandable if you're not. I don't know how you must be feeling after what happened yesterday. I know you know this, but please feel free to talk with me if you need and want to, Dublin. I'm just concerned about all this, but mostly I'm worried about *you*. I love you, son."

Andy's words spilled out rapidly, but as always, they were genuine and filled with compassion. Dublin looked over at his papa and, straightening in his saddle, winced slightly. "I love you, too. And I'm sure. Don't worry about me, Papa. Now, I'll admit I *am* concerned about that strange man crossing both of our paths again and what he could potentially do. But as for what has already happened, right now at least, I'm fine. I truly feel alright. The pain is nothing worse than anything else I have ever had to deal with. I'm just trying to convince myself to remember that God is in control and to just hold on to the knowledge that He will see us through anything, to just have faith."

Nodding in understanding, Andy held the boy's gaze. "Well, I understand what you mean, son. Just because I've been a Christian longer than you doesn't mean I've mastered the ability to not worry or that I always trust God. I know and believe that God has us safely in His hands, even now. We'll have to see what Sheriff Walters has to say. Maybe he'll know who that man is. Needless to say, I am relieved that you are feeling fairly well, all things considered. And I'll do whatever I can to ensure your safety. I've basically been in a constant state of prayer in my heart, asking for God's protection for you, for the both of us. Hopefully, before long this won't even be a concern of ours."

Andy smiled over at Dublin. In return, the boy offered a brave, convincing grin his father's way. They quieted down again, urging their horses into a laid-back trot until they came to the town. At that point, they reined their horses back to a slow walk.

The town of London was not particularly busy since it was still rather early. It wasn't even quite 8:00 a.m. School wouldn't begin for the students for more than an hour, and while some businesses were already open for the first workday of the week, the town was still relatively peaceful.

Making their way to the sheriff's office, which included a small jail on the premises, father and son rode their horses toward the hitching posts outside the jail, promptly dismounting. They tied their stallions to the posts securely. Micah and Fareed just stood there, seemingly content. Andy and Dublin wandered nervously into the building.

Sheriff Daniel Walters was sitting at his desk, apparently buried in a steep pile of paperwork. It was nice to see not a single soul in any of the jail cells behind his desk, even though there was an unnamed, unknown man who *needed* to be there in a cell, locked up for their safety.

Sheriff Walters looked up from his tasks and smiled easily, recognizing Andy Caldwell and his boy. But he frowned just as quickly as he looked more closely at the teenager. Dublin's face was badly bruised and scraped on the right side.

"Good morning, gentlemen," the sheriff greeted them warmly. He extended his hand, and both of them took turns shaking it firmly. "Dublin, what's happened?" he asked, concern in his voice.

Dublin relayed all the distressing details of the previous day's sinister events to Sheriff Walters, who listened intently. Discernible contempt could be seen across the sheriff's features toward the dangerous, nameless man.

CHAPTER FIVE

"Well, boys, I can assure you both that I will be on the lookout for anyone who could be our man," Sheriff Walters replied indignantly. He appeared to be quite perturbed. "But from your description of him, I don't know his name. I mean, he doesn't sound like anybody I have been trying to track down who has committed other crimes. I will do all I can to bring him in. In the meantime, please be alert, both of you.

"And please take special care to be *very* cautious. I'd recommend that you take care and not ride alone on your property since that was where Dublin was shot and he was alone when it happened. You may not even want to ride together on your land, not until this man is brought in and brought to justice. Just be safe and careful. And Andy, you already know this, for I see your gun holstered on you now, but keep that gun of yours on you for protection at all times, at least until this is resolved."

Andy nodded slowly while the sheriff spoke. "Yes, I certainly agree," Andy answered. "We'll be cautious. And I appreciate your time and help with this matter. I pray you'll be able to apprehend him before too long. I thank you for your time, Daniel. You have been a wonderful sheriff to the town of London for the past year and a half. God bless you and your excellent deputies. Thank you again."

He shook Sheriff Walters's hand once more. Dublin followed suit. Then Dublin and Andy headed out of the building to allow the sheriff to return to his paperwork.

"Well, even though we don't know anything now," Andy said to Dublin, "at least the sheriff is aware of the situation. I trust he'll be on the lookout and that he'll find that man so before too much longer he will no longer be a threat. I just hope, for your sake, that it is very soon. Your peace of mind is probably not at one hundred percent right now, huh?"

Dublin hesitated before truthfully shaking his head. "No, Papa, it isn't. But I'm not altogether worried sick, either, at least not consciously. I do have a feeling that this will turn out alright. I just don't know when or how or what must happen in order for things to work out in our favor."

Andy was amazed by his son's wisdom for still being a teenager. But he had to remind himself that Dublin was nearly grown. Dublin was now much more of a positive being, not one to dwell so much anymore on negativity or his past to the point of making himself miserable, scared, or sick. He was maturing into a respectable young man. Andy couldn't have been any happier about that.

Climbing aboard their mounts, they reined the stallions back toward their home. Both had fleeting thoughts of how nice it would be to ride through the woods on this particularly beautiful day, but neither wished to foolishly risk an unnecessary encounter with yesterday's gunman, whoever he was. They began riding toward the town's limits and on toward their home when abruptly a shot was fired. It echoed in the distance. Then they both heard the sound of horses' hooves drumming rapidly against the hard dirt path that led to London. Straining to hear more sounds such as yelling—anything at all—they remained motionless and quiet. But they heard nothing else for a short while.

Soon, though, they could tell that the sound of hoofbeats drumming hard upon the ground was becoming louder. The unknown riders were drawing ever closer. Andy quickly motioned for Dublin to move off the dirt road, out of the riders' way. All of a sudden, a horse and rider came into sight. Andy recognized the man instantly, first by his Appaloosa horse and second by his short-cropped, black hair. Carter Fallon!

This is unusual, Andy thought. *Why would Fallon be coming into town from the west, from near my property? He never comes out my way.*

Then something indicating impending doom rather than being merely perplexing came into view. Fallon's pursuer rode into sight. Though Andy had never seen this man before, he knew from deep within that this was the very same person who'd shot his son.

The man was very tall and broad, certainly a foreboding figure. He rode a deep-bay draft-horse cross, perhaps a Percheron crossed with a Thoroughbred, or maybe even an American Saddlebred. The horse was huge but not as massive as a full-blooded Percheron would have been. Its warm-blood descent helped make the horse tall and fast for its great width. And this horse was galloping full-speed in hot pursuit of Carter Fallon. Its rider aimed not a rifle at Fallon but instead a handgun resembling a newer Schofield revolver.

Fallon's Appaloosa mare strained as she ran at top speed. Despite her valiant efforts, he relentlessly kicked at her sides, urging her faster and faster in his desperation to escape unharmed. They streaked by Andy and Dublin in a blurry flash. Andy quickly drew his gun, thinking mainly of protecting his son. But he was also responding in part to his anger toward this unknown man who was charging toward them. He also felt the need to keep his long-time adversary from being shot to death.

Andy aimed his trusty Colt revolver and then fired. The bullet made its way to his intended target, propelling the unidentified man's Schofield from his right hand. The big, burly man cried out from the forceful removal of his gun he'd been holding with a death grip. His large horse reared and promptly bucked, thus throwing him off its back.

Carter Fallon didn't see what happened, but he heard Andy's shot ring out through the woods. He was blissfully unaware that it was the man he hated most whose bullet had likely saved his life. He reined his mare around, riding her back toward the two riders at the side of the road. He went toward his former friend—the large, now-unarmed man.

This man had turned on Carter and threatened to take his life when he wouldn't agree to help him kill Andrew Caldwell and his son. It was all so this man—Harvey Adamson—could steal Andy's horses, unhindered, and sell them for a huge profit.

Carter could not understand why Adamson had wanted Andy's horses in the first place. It was his opinion that his Arabians were too small and rather high-strung. When Harvey Adamson had come to Carter not long ago with his proposal that Carter and Harvey work together to kill Andy and Dublin Caldwell, he had offered to give him a bounteous portion of the large sum of money they'd surely make from selling all 16 of Andy's horses, not to mention the money they may well discover in the old farmhouse.

Carter, though he was a generally mean-spirited and short-tempered man, one who held on to grudges, found it easy to adamantly refuse Adamson's offer. For while he had a rather short fuse and was reluctant to forgive, he was *not* a murderer. He told Harvey he would have no part of the proposition.

Now, Harvey Adamson struggled to pick himself up off the dusty ground. When he'd fallen from his steed, his ankle had broken. He swore furiously and then looked up at the two silent riders—both of them his intended victims, no less—and his raging hazel eyes narrowed into thin slits. His firearm was nowhere within his reach. He cursed again.

Carter Fallon halted his horse beside Andy and Dublin. He felt his skin crawl with disgust being this close to the double reasons he'd been removed from his school teaching position three years ago. And while he basically hated those two goody-two-shoes, he couldn't bring himself to continue hating these gentlemen after what they'd just done on his behalf—for saving his life.

But he couldn't bring himself to thank them, either. That would simply be too much. He could appreciate the favor without liking them. He merely regarded the Caldwell man and boy silently before turning his attention to the large man lying crumpled on the ground, swearing at him profusely.

"Carter Fallon, you are the biggest coward in this town," Harvey Adamson spat brutally. "The likes of you ought to be put out of their misery."

Carter hardly winced. He was accustomed to verbal abuse from others, namely from his mother and stepfather. But there were others who had bullied him throughout his wretched, pointless existence, an existence he seemed to be desperately trying to preserve even though it was so miserable and useless.

"Adamson, you just hush up, right now," Fallon growled bitterly. "To think you were once my friend, and now you've tried to kill me. Well, that didn't work, so now you're resorting to insulting me. Shut up, and hold still. I'll show you what a coward is capable of."

Andy and Dublin stared at them in disbelief. It was hard to believe that this murderous man Adamson and Carter Fallon were once friends. Even Andy knew something respectable surely lay beneath Carter Fallon's tough exterior. He believed his brusque and intolerant facade belied a man who certainly was not murderous, not like the one lying on the ground.

They watched, open-mouthed, as Carter hopped off his Appaloosa mare, ground-hitching her, and then pulled out some rough lengths of rope from one of his saddlebags. Harvey Adamson shifted his attention to the ones he'd truly wanted to kill, his expression dark.

"You boys sure are lucky with how things are turning out," Harvey grunted. "Had it gone my way, that youngster would already be dead, and I would have gone through with shooting *you* dead, and cowardly Carter here, too, the worthless idiot that he is. You'll all live to regret interfering with my plans, you hear?" He struggled against Fallon, who was able to tightly tie his large hands at the wrists and behind his back.

"All of you!" Adamson continued his hollering. "*All* of you will regret turning me in. I'll seek vengeance on each one of you once I find my way outta that there jail in town. This I promise."

"Sir," Andy shot back, "I don't even want to know why you were planning on killing my son and me, but I assure you that whatever it is, it's completely unfounded. But you won't escape from that jail. And if you think that Sheriff Walters is going to up and release you anytime soon, you're sorely mistaken. He will see to it that you're in there for a long time for attempted murder on my son and now Mr. Fallon here."

Harvey Adamson scoffed. "You may never comprehend my reasoning, but you're wrong. I *will* get out of there."

Carter pulled his former friend up to his feet, and Harvey Adamson promptly cursed from the pain as he placed his weight on his broken ankle in an attempt to stay upright on his own. Fallon dragged Adamson, limping badly, over to his draft-cross horse and helped him mount the huge animal. Harvey settled roughly on the gelding's oversized English saddle, still spewing hateful profanity. Then Carter Fallon faced both of his least-favorite residents in the entire town of London—in any town, for that matter. And he smiled.

Andy was taken aback but perhaps not as much as Dublin was. They just stared at Carter, open-mouthed and in disbelief. Andy, with a genuine smile on his face, finally spoke to Carter Fallon. Everyone ignored the bound man who refused to cease his spiteful cursing.

"Glad you are alright, Fallon. Why don't you come with us to see Sheriff Walters so you can help fill him in on whatever this nonsense is that's going on. Would you, please?"

It is simply Papa's nature to be a gentleman, Dublin thought, observing Andy and Mr. Fallon. His tongue caught in his mouth, currently paralyzed, while his papa spoke to the historically unkind but now-smiling man.

Carter nodded slowly. "Yeah, I suppose I ought to, Caldwell. Oh, by the way, thank you for uh...saving my life," he replied awkwardly.

Andy offered him an easy smile, nodding. "My pleasure. That man right there is responsible for injuring my son. He shot Dublin yesterday, but thank God, the bullet merely grazed him. He wasn't seriously injured. So what do you say we get him over to the sheriff's office and into a jail cell?"

"Let's go," Carter Fallon said promptly. He mounted his Appaloosa mare, taking hold of Harvey Adamson's reins in his own hand to lead the irate but now silent, bound man along the road into town. They made meager small talk along the way to see the sheriff, and it remarkably wasn't altogether too awkward. Andy felt a small spark rise in his big heart, and it told him that maybe all Carter Fallon had needed all along was a real friend. He supposed that despite his own hesitations, he could easily fill that role and be the stern man's friend.

It may change Carter's demeanor, entirely, he thought. *There's always hope.*

CHAPTER SIX

With the suspect in custody and safely behind bars—complete with charges brought against him that were of no little matter, the three who'd brought the man to the jail all exited the building together. Sheriff Walters had assured them that Harvey Adamson would be in there securely for a long while.

Dublin remained quiet. He felt apprehensive of Carter Fallon, his former school teacher who'd threatened him once when he was 14. He would have preferred to just avoid him altogether. But he could tell as he and his papa spent more time in his company that his desire probably wasn't likely going to be a possibility. Nope.

"Say, Carter, how would you like to have some lunch over at our place?" Andy suddenly found himself inviting the formerly austere man to his home for a meal together, the man who was displaying more normal and gentler behaviors by the minute. Andy wondered how Dublin felt about that.

Well, we all have to give folks more than one chance, Andy rationalized in his mind. *Carter Fallon was nearly killed today, and he seems somewhat of a different man now, nicer even. He doesn't have any relatives around here, and if that Adamson man was his friend, then he doesn't have any idea what good friends truly are. We ought to give him another chance, and hopefully, Dublin will understand and forgive me for making him uncomfortable, as he surely must be right now.*

Carter Fallon glanced curiously over at Andy Caldwell. Certainly, Andy knew how Carter had hated him, and Andy was surely not fond of him, either. So why the invitation all of a sudden?

Even though Carter couldn't fathom Andy's reasoning, he found himself agreeing. "Sure, Caldwell, a nice meal sounds good right about now. Thank you kindly."

Carter didn't bother to try to conceal the confusion in his voice. The truth was that it was entirely foreign to him to be talking so pleasantly with this man.

"You're most welcome, Carter. I have some pretty decent leftovers from yesterday's lunch that I hope you might like. Fish and fried potatoes, and some canned peas I can warm up, too. How does that sound?"

Fallon shrugged, but honestly, he thought it sounded superb. He felt he needed to rein in all this friendliness or else he was going to end up liking this Caldwell man. He wasn't certain if he wanted to like him or not, but it was becoming evident that he was starting to, regardless of wanting to. He offered him an easy smile and a reply.

"Yeah, that's fine, Caldwell." Carter then glanced over at Andy who was riding alongside him off to his left side, smiling and looking pleased. He couldn't figure out why Andy was being so kind to him. Andy glanced over at him, noting a distinct look of pain in the man's gray eyes. He wondered about the source. Everyone has a story. But now was not the time to ask about it and consequently chase the man off when they were just becoming civil human beings to each other.

"Wonderful!" Andy exclaimed.

They made their way to Andy's farm just in time to see young Akilah start bucking like a little rodeo pony. Cameron, one of Andy's employees, was hanging on for dear life. He'd been thrown from young horses a few times in the past few years, but right now, he was clinging to that filly's sturdy back like she had adhesive all over her back.

Upon closer inspection, however, it really didn't look like it was all that simple. The expression on Cameron's face revealed that he was giving it his all to keep on the young horse's back. Finally, Akilah claimed victory over the well-fought tussle, and Cameron landed hard on the ground, right on his seat.

"Ooh!" he exclaimed, as he collided with the hard ground. He coughed, struggled to his feet, and then dusted off his pants. He soon smiled, signaling that he was alright.

The other hired hands struggled to get the agitated horse under control and reasonably calmed down. The young Arabian was full of spirit and fire. At first, she fought the lead rope with all her might. Finally, though, she allowed the men to get her halted, and then she stood there, tail off to the side and docile as though nothing had happened at all.

Andy called out to Les and asked him for help unsaddling all three horses, giving the men a respite of sorts after their wild and frightening ride and allowing Andy and Dublin to visit with and ultimately get Carter Fallon and themselves fed.

Andy hadn't realized how ravenously hungry he was. They'd all been at the sheriff's office until nearly 1:00 that afternoon, missing his and Dublin's usual lunchtime. Skipping dinner last night probably didn't help any, either. It was now past 1:30 p.m., and everyone's stomachs were growling in anticipation of some lunch.

Dublin still hadn't said a word. He could feel prickly little hairs standing up at the back of his neck, even though his former teacher was clearly exhibiting some modified, much more pleasant mannerisms.

But can I really trust him?

Andy suggested that Carter tie his Appaloosa mare named Seneca to the iron bars of Marguerite's stall. Andy gave Seneca a bucket of cool water and a pile of fresh hay. Carter quietly thanked him for providing for his horse. He was truly grateful and humbled. Then they all went inside.

Dublin wordlessly assisted his papa with preparing and heating up their lunch. Andy could sense his son's evident discomfort, but he didn't quite feel it was appropriate to say anything soothing to him about Mr. Fallon in front of Mr. Fallon, no less. So he chose to always position himself between Fallon and Dublin at all times to silently reassure his son that Mr. Fallon would have to go through him to cause him any harm. Even so, Andy didn't feel like Fallon was a threat—not anymore.

Dublin picked up on his father's silent message, but he still felt rather uneasy. Interestingly, though, he was curious about the man. And that was interesting because his curiosity couldn't be explained.

The two men and the boy sat at the table as Andy and Dublin bowed their heads for prayer. Carter Fallon remained in his normal sitting position in defiance against praying to God whom he felt had failed him for the duration of his entire, miserable life.

God is probably just a fictitious being, anyway, Fallon grumbled in his heart.

Andy and Dublin simultaneously said amen and then looked up. Carter tentatively grasped his fork and began to take small bites of his blackened trout, which, he had to admit, was quite good. It had an excellent flavor, and the seasoning was perfect. As he continued eating, Carter noted with pleasure that he liked everything else, too. It was all much better than what Carter was capable of cooking at his place.

Dublin sat rigidly, totally uncomfortable with Mr. Fallon sitting off to his one side, but he knew Andy's generous, loving, forgiving heart and that even a man such as Mr. Fallon would never be exempt from Andy's graciousness. Besides, Dublin would never verbally oppose his papa's decision to have the historically snide, surly man in their home and at their table. He doubted if Mr. Fallon would make an attempt to harm him in any way. But he still didn't know that with absolute certainty. That, in turn, wavered his confidence, so he kept stealing wary glances at the thin but certainly strong man, making certain that he would not strike at him. He felt rather silly about his wariness, but he simply couldn't help himself.

Feeling uneasy, Dublin finished his meal. He was greatly tempted to ask to be excused since he'd finished eating ahead of both his papa and Fallon. He was also beginning to feel rather light-headed. But he didn't ask. He wouldn't. He just sat there almost as though he were frozen in place, dazed. Then the moment he'd feared came.

Suddenly, Carter Fallon's right hand shot out toward Dublin. Dublin recoiled, panic-stricken, but he couldn't stop himself. That's when he realized he was beginning to faint. Mr. Fallon's strong hand grasped Dublin's left shoulder and his shirt. He was able to catch the boy before he fell heavily to the hardwood floor. So there, cradled in the arms of the least likely of men, was Dublin Caldwell, passed out cold.

Carter looked down curiously at the pale teen. Then he looked at Andy. "Is he alright?" he found himself asking with concern, still supporting the teenager's limp body.

Andy nodded slowly, rushing to his son's side. He pressed his palm against the boy's forehead. It felt cool and clammy. Then he felt the boy's cheeks, and Dublin stirred, though he remained unconscious.

"He'll be fine, Carter. He's been known to become so worked up or stressed about some things that he grows too overwhelmed, and then he just up and passes out."

Guilt flashed through Fallon's heart and soul. Andy didn't have to say it. He knew he was the cause of the teenage boy's distress. He knew it. And he felt remorseful.

"I'm sorry, Andy. I'm sure this is my fault," Carter said forlornly and with much resignation. The melancholy in his voice did not go unnoticed.

Andy felt overcome with sympathy for this man. "Now, Carter, Dublin is going to be just fine. But I think maybe the two of you need to have a brand-new perspective on each other, a new and improved introduction. I mean, you have to know he didn't deserve the punishment you were about to give him one day a few years ago. Am I correct?" Andy gave the man holding on to his son rather tenderly and concernedly a stern and reproving look.

Fallon bowed his head shamefully. Though he wouldn't meet Andy Caldwell's gaze, he did respond with a slow, nearly imperceptible nod. He sighed. "Yes, I realize that."

"Good. Then maybe a bit after he awakens, you might consider apologizing to him. You really ought to know that this boy is as kind and respectable as they come, and he's not ill-mannered in any way. You might even like him if you get to know him," Andy replied, his voice trailing off but still holding a certain firmness.

Andy said a quick, silent prayer that the man would find peace in whatever way or ways he needed and some much-needed joy in his life.

"I know I should apologize," Fallon added. "I behaved unacceptably. I took out my disdain and resentment for you on him once I surmised the boy was your adopted son, however that came to be. I knew he was not your boy by blood, and I took that opportunity to try to make him look the fool and as an opportunity to punish him. I'd had a rather unpleasant morning, and in those days, giving him a taste of my switch would have been satisfactory to me and probably would have assuaged my bitterness.

"But today, now I see the error of my ways with him and the other children, too. I know that giving him a switching wouldn't have ultimately helped me feel any better. I suppose, though, that my incorrect thinking at the time and in times since of varying sorts to this day have my boyhood to blame. Not that it gives me any legitimate excuse for how I have acted."

Carter could hardly restrain his tongue as he opened up to the man he thought he'd hated the most. Andy cocked his head off to one side ever so slightly, frowning with concern for Carter Fallon. Adversary or not, Carter currently seemed like a friend intent on sharing with Andy his darkest secrets. It was strange but refreshing how God could take certain situations and turn them on end for the better. Carter was still a living, breathing, hurting human being—and evidently with a past.

Carter Fallon bowed his head and then, before he could help himself, found himself brushing his right hand tenderly across the unconscious boy's cheek. Andy was full of all sorts of conflicting emotions, but they were mainly good. He allowed a small smile to play at the corners of his mouth. Suddenly, Fallon began sharing even more with Andy.

"I had a rough childhood, Caldwell. I didn't live around here growing up else you would have already known about it probably. I, uh, haven't told another soul in years. My father was a good man, but he died when I was 12. My mama, she never recovered from his death. She changed into a completely different person. She soon became mean-spirited, constantly criticizing me the moment my father passed away. Never was she supportive, not ever, once he was gone.

"Then she began seeing a man who quickly became her new husband. He treated her reasonably well, but as for me, well, not really. Mr. Hanover, as he was called, was not against slapping me for any infraction, failure, or whatever. Sometimes I had not even done anything wrong, and he would hit me full force in the face. That soon progressed to beatings with whatever he could find nearby. He was very volatile.

"Mr. Hanover died two years later before I was old enough to start out on my own. And then my mother passed away shortly after. I was left with my younger brother and sisters. They were sent to my mother's sister's home, but I wanted nothing to do with that, so I ran away. At just 14, I lived on my own until I was able to attend college. I became the schoolmaster here in London after being one in a nearby town for many years after my college graduation. I was let go there, and Caldwell, that wasn't my fault. It was because that town wanted to hire someone new and pay him or her less.

"I was furious and embittered, rightfully so, I think. Since I was in a worse frame of mind than ever, I was not apt to take any misdeeds from any student and would punish them with a switch to show them I was not against putting them in their places. I also did that to serve as an example to the other children for better, all-around behavior. For the most part, it worked, keeping the others out of trouble except for one student, Samuel Geoffreys. He always pushed my buttons and seemed to lack the sense to learn from his mistakes. So I felt rather compelled to give him his share of switchings."

Carter had shared truthfully with Andy without much hesitation in his voice. Andy had listened closely, growing quite somber over the information that Fallon had for some reason decided to share with him—information he felt he could trust him with. Andy shook his head sadly.

"Carter, I am sorry to hear about your past and all your pain and disappointments, as well as your struggles. Don't take me the wrong way, but while they don't *excuse* your actions toward the students and my son, they do *explain* them. And for that explanation, I am truly grateful. You've had a rough way of it on this road called life, and again, I am so very sorry.

"You did *not* deserve those things that happened to you. I hope you realize that. And I do see a strongly rooted tenderness within you right now with my son in your arms. I hope that since you trusted me with all this information, you and I might become friends. I, at least, would like that very much. What do you say about that, Carter?"

Carter Fallon met Andy's kind, brown gaze, and with his shoulders hunched forward, he found himself in easy agreement.

"I would like that, too, Caldwell. It just isn't worthwhile to hate and harbor resentment toward someone else, especially when you saved my life. And Andy, I *know* that horse you sold me years ago was in excellent condition. It was me who failed to care for his feet. I know you did not sell him to me lame. I'm sorry I chose to place the blame on you and try to give you a bad reputation around the town of London.

"Please, I hope you'll forgive me. I was terribly wrong in what I did. I don't deserve to be considered your friend, but I hope someday I will be. It would bring me some happiness to have a friend in this world. It would perhaps make life more bearable to have a good man like you as a friend, someone who is on my side and not in direct opposition to me."

Andy placed his broad hand across the man's hunched shoulders. "All is forgiven. After seeing you catch my son and hold him so gently, I'd venture to say that, in my opinion, you definitely deserve to be my friend. Anyone who is kind to my son is alright in my book." Andy winked at his last comment.

Carter found himself smiling a hesitant but authentic smile. His heart warmed with validation as a natural result of Andy's kindhearted, easygoing nature—of Andy's forgiveness.

CHAPTER SEVEN

Dublin awoke with a start, realizing at once that again he'd passed out from becoming so overwhelmed by distress about something. It had certainly been stressful being so close to Mr. Carter Fallon.

He awoke to discover with fright that he was even closer to him. He was lying in Fallon's arms. Dublin's sapphire eyes widened even more, and he nearly jumped right out of Mr. Fallon's lap, clearly panic-stricken. Thankfully, as a 17-year-old, he didn't scream or cry like a weak, fearful, little child, although he easily could have. Biting his tongue with fierce willpower, he whirled around, jumped to his feet, and ran to safety across the room. He glared at Carter Fallon with intense, distrusting eyes.

Andy watched him with at least some level of sympathetic understanding as well as some slight amusement for his boy's reaction. Fallon stared at Dublin in consternation. Now he *did* understand that the teenager was fearful of him and was well aware that he also disliked him. But Fallon was stubbornly unconvinced that Dublin's reactions just now were altogether called for.

"Now hang on, Dublin. Get a hold of yourself," Fallon commented in the form of a more brusque command than he'd meant for it to be. "I'm not going to harm you," he added in a milder tone.

Dublin just stared at him in utter disbelief, his mouth agape. Confusion took hold of him.

Mr. Fallon continued. "You fainted, and I caught you. Your father and I were just talking, and I feel I ought to offer you a sincere apology finally for how I treated you and spoke to you back when you were in my classroom. It wasn't right. I do realize that. Please, would you forgive me? Andy and I are interested in becoming friends instead of foolishly remaining enemies for stupid reasons. And I hope that you and I will be able to get along, too," Fallon explained, sounding to Dublin as if he meant every word.

But how can I trust this man? Dublin wondered.

Regardless of his doubts, Dublin found himself nodding slowly. "I forgive you, Mr. Fallon. If my father wants to become friends with you, then I trust his judgment," he said simply, although he had to restrain himself from spitefully adding *even if I don't understand his way of thinking.*

Dublin offered the tiniest of smiles, not entirely certain it was 100 percent genuine, but he was trying. Mr. Fallon's expression displayed evident relief, and he exhaled. Then he smiled and proceeded to offer his large right hand to Dublin. The teenager bravely took it in his own without hesitation. They shook hands amicably. Andy observed, his expression revealing obvious pleasure. His new friend was, in turn, making friends with his son.

> *Wow! Whoever would have guessed that this would be happening now, right here in my own kitchen? Praise God that He's helped turn a former enemy into a friend. Lord, please bless our friendship with Carter Fallon, and bless him. He could use the blessing—some good things in life. And if he knows not Your Son, please help me share the gospel with him in a way that he might understand someday when he is receptive. For no one but Jesus alone can heal Carter's broken heart and his troubled life. In Jesus's name. Amen.*

Peace settling into his heart, Andy suggested to Carter and Dublin that they go check on his hired hands to see how they were coming along training the horses, especially Kamaria. Perhaps they could go for a leisurely ride afterward since the woodlands were now safe, at least from Harvey Adamson.

Carter readily agreed since he didn't have any work today. He also hadn't a thing waiting for him at home, save for maybe a half-drunk bottle or time he would spend utterly alone ruminating on all the things that were wrong in his life, currently and also in the past—a past from which he could never quite fully escape.

Dublin agreed, and the three of them wandered outdoors and over toward the training paddock. The men had the beautiful Kamaria under saddle, and she was fully bridled. She seemed a bit unhappy with a saddle on her back, and she kept trying to wriggle out from under it. But she repeatedly found out that she couldn't do so successfully. So she began bucking. Les called out to Frederick, who held on to her lead rope with fervor. He spoke to her with gentle reassurance and attempted to calm her down by pulling with a controlled firmness on her lead rope that was attached to her halter and clipped to an O-ring underneath her bit and bridle.

Les Morrison instructed his subordinate, who was much older and more seasoned than he was, on how to handle the horse. "Freddy, just go ahead and let go of her for a bit, would you? Let her get used to the sensation of having a saddle on her back, a bridle on her head, a bit in her mouth, and so on. Do that for a while and then try to teach her all the cues and how to respond appropriately."

Freddy harbored no hard feelings toward Les who had been given the supervising position. Leslie Morrison was a good, able-bodied, intelligent horseman, and he was *always* dependable. He deserved the position he had held now for about three years.

Freddy had no problem obeying the younger man's instructions. They were sensible, after all. Freddy also liked that if Les gave directions that he happened to disagree with or knew better about, he could talk it over with Les. Sometimes, Freddy's better judgment and methods were used instead.

Freddy released his hold on the filly's lead rope. Then surprisingly, the filly started toward Freddy, who was able to unclip her lead rope from her purple halter. The young, spirited horse tossed her head and pranced about, eventually slowing down to a much calmer walk around the training paddock until finally she slowed to a stop, standing peacefully.

Les cautioned the men to give Kamaria several more minutes to herself before approaching her and working with her again. They easily agreed with his direction.

Andy and his son, as well as their newfound friend, just stood, watching, captivated by the filly's antics. After Freddy taught the young filly how to stop as her reins were pulled back, the first cue he taught her, Andy finally pulled himself away, encouraging his two companions to join him in saddling some horses.

Carter's horse was already saddled, but Andy's and Dublin's weren't. So they busied themselves while Carter observed, standing near his beautiful, mottled Appaloosa mare. Dublin decided, out of ease, to resaddle Micah since Mr. Fallon's horse was tied to Marguerite's stall and would be in the way of saddling Marguerite. There would be no guarantee that plenty of room would be left over for comfort's sake—comfort that he would not be too close to Mr. Fallon.

Fallon was slowly proving to Dublin that he had kindly intentions toward him and his papa. Dublin truly wished to be friends, but it was an altogether puzzling realization. Was it really possible for seemingly hardhearted men to just up and change their behaviors, as well as their ways of thinking or acting? Could they act like halfway decent, respectable men who could perhaps be trusted?

Well, apparently it is possible for this man to change, Dublin sternly told himself, trying to convince himself enough to depart from his nagging doubts. He finished tightening the girth for the last time on Micah's saddle before readjusting the stirrups slightly to the best length for him. They'd become stretched a little too much somewhere along the way since earlier in the day.

"That's a fine-looking horse you have there, Dublin," Carter Fallon couldn't resist commenting from behind. Dublin was currently fully focused on his tasks at hand. Jumping ever so slightly, the boy whirled around to face his former teacher. He was the one he'd feared as his student and begrudged quite a bit over the years. Regardless, Dublin recovered, offering him a tentative approving smile.

"Well, thank you, Mr. Fallon," he replied, warmed by the man's compliment that sounded genuine. Dublin did not want his horses to be revered by others; however, he enjoyed the fact that he had Mr. Fallon's honest approval of his stallion.

"He's been a fine, sound mount while I've had him," Dublin added. Papa and I have bred him with some of the Quarter Horse mares, and he's even bred with one Arabian, though that was not our intention. Marisah is not due for another two months, but I, for one, am curious to see the foal once it's born. Marisah's out to pasture so you cannot see her right this moment, but she is a Palomino. The foal ought to come out pretty, but it's anyone's guess what it will look like or which breed it'll favor," he explained, glad to share the exciting information with even Carter Fallon, who was still continuing to show his softer side.

Maybe he will be alright after all, Dublin thought. *I can't believe I am thinking this, but I actually hope we do become good friends.*

Dublin proceeded to mount his stallion as soon as his papa was astride the horse he'd saddled. Predictably, he sat on his good, old, faithful black horse. Not to be left out, Carter smiled slightly before he climbed aboard Seneca.

Soon, the three of them were off, heading outdoors from inside the barn. They ambled down a well-beaten path in Andy's woods, all of them silently taking in the universally green scenery. Though it was made up of vastly diverse shrubbery, trees, and flowers, the scenery all seemed to blend together into a single, large, green sight before them. Occasionally, vibrantly colored flowers colorfully dotted the foliage around them in an intricately interlocking manner, complete with their beauty.

Carter sat atop his pretty mare and stretched his legs downward in the stirrups. He was becoming rather comfortable in the company of Andy and his son. Just riding along among the gorgeous scenery, rocks, hills, and trees—all there was to Andy's captivating woods—added to his relaxed state the farther they ventured. He felt a strong, budding companionship with these two, and though it was truly confusing—preposterous, almost—he was grateful for it. He couldn't have been even a tad happier had he been elsewhere and left to his obsessive thoughts, his default negativity rooted deeply in his troubled mind.

Andy and Dublin ended up taking him to the Teays River by the father-son pair's favorite fishing spot. The three of them ground-hitched their horses by the shady, welcoming willow tree while the horses grazed at will, side by side and content. Then the gentlemen walked from the willow tree to the river's edge where the two stumps were. They were both still there. Andy had placed them there for him and his late wife—his love, Addalyn Caldwell, his dear, sweet Addie. She'd died during childbirth some time before Dublin came into the picture.

Andy's thoughts wandered. *It was time to give birth to the child we had been impatiently and excitedly expecting for what felt like an eternity, with unrestrained joy, but Addie didn't make it. And the daughter we'd both longed for was stillborn. I never held her in my arms while she had life within her. I would never know the color of her eyes for they were sealed— closed—as though she was merely sleeping. But of course, she wasn't breathing, either. Oh, Isabelle.*

Andy felt the familiar pain and tears resurfacing, crashing all about him mercilessly while he recalled the two lost loves of his life who could never return to him, not until he breathed his last and joined them in heaven one day.

But, he reminded himself in a silent, sharp, chastising tone in his mind, *now you have Dublin. And he has been a wonderful son to you. Remember how blessed you actually are, Caldwell.*

He remained quiet as he, Carter, and Dublin made their way over to the two stumps. Offering them to his son and his new friend, Andy chose to remain standing, a tall but vulnerable figure. At least, he *felt* incredibly vulnerable at the present moment. Dublin noticed Andy's solemnity right away. He knew the origin of it but thought it wise to avoid mentioning his papa's late wife and daughter.

Deep down, Carter had a sensitive soul that lay beneath a rough exterior. So he, too, noticed Andy's shift in demeanor, his acute onset of melancholy. But he said nothing and didn't react, staying true to his historically tough facade. Deep inside, though, he felt curious about the sudden, drastic change in the tall man's conduct. Andy had always seemed so confident and content. But now, a sadness lingered across all his strong features.

The three men stared out across the flowing river, each in their own respective state of brokenness, reminiscing of loves lost, love that never existed but should have, and pain, just utter pain, disappointment, and heartbreak.

Enthralled by the wind blowing about his face, Andy felt like he was in a trance. Standing there tall, still, and silent, he was lost in his thoughts, entranced totally by the rhythmic wind that continuously assailed his face a little more than gently. Finally, the silence was broken by the sound of one of the men speaking. Dublin looked over to Carter Fallon, the one who was talking.

"I truly appreciate the kindness, patience, and assistance, among other things, you boys have shown me today," Carter said, his gaze far away and directed across the river somewhere. "Even though I don't deserve your friendship, I am glad for it and for your forgiveness especially. You two are the only kind faces I have seen in an awfully long time, and you have been willing to invest time and energy in me."

While the handyman sounded hopelessly dejected, a faint but detectable glimmer of hope was in his voice. It was as though he could recognize Andy's and Dublin's efforts, their easy friendships. He truly was consciously grateful for both of them. But the fact remained that he currently had no one else in his life who cared. To Carter, that realization was disheartening. It also somehow offered a faint but fortified glimpse of a fresh, new dawn breaking brightly across the dark, stormy skies looming over his life. It was a dawn that aimed to cover his bleak existence with the brilliance of true friendship, these kind people now involved in his life.

Andy, emotion tugging at the corners of his heart, reached down and laid his large hand on Fallon's left shoulder, comfortingly saying, "It'll all be alright, Carter." He paused for several moments. "I don't know how or when, but God will see to it. He will either change your circumstances or change you to help you scale all the looming mountains in your life, raising you up to see that the Lord indeed is good and faithful. You will see that there is always hope in all situations. He won't leave you alone to take care of all your problems on your own but rather will see to it that you grow and find peace and happiness."

Unfortunately, Carter did not respond favorably. "Caldwell," he snapped, reverting to his former temperament upon hearing Andy's words about God, a being he hadn't any use for. "Keep your God talk to yourself. God has not been present in my life thus far, and I have no desire to come crawling to Him admitting I've failed and sinned when it's God who has abandoned me and forgotten me. He's never come to my aid, not even when I've needed Him the most. I don't need preached to. I can survive just fine in this life without being preached to by some man who foolishly trusts in an unseen God while not really knowing if He's even there."

Dublin stared at him, open-mouthed. He was completely taken aback by Mr. Fallon's response, which wasn't kind by any means. He truly didn't know if he was going to be able to trust the stern man whose demeanor could shift at the proverbial flip of a coin.

Andy was not shocked—not really—yet he, too, stared speechlessly, although only for a brief moment. Then he offered him a reply, attempting to placate the riled man.

"Carter, my apologies to you for coming across like I was preaching to you. I can certainly appreciate where you're coming from—your doubts and hesitations toward God. I know I have not been in your shoes, but I have been where I felt like God was absent in my life, as though He was uncaring and unloving. But let me assure you, He *is* here, and He *does* love you—dearly—enough to have His Son die for the sins of all the people in the world. I won't press you anymore about it, I promise. But *please*, let's be amicable. I still want greatly to be your friend, Carter," Andy said gently.

Carter glanced up at him and rose from his stump abruptly. He pushed up his shirt sleeves, which to Dublin was a frightening indication that the man likely wanted to initiate a fight against his papa.

Carter Fallon, changed or not, certainly has enough of a mean streak in him to start a brawl, thought Dublin.

A growing sense of apprehension arose inside Dublin's chest as he began to feel distressed and faint once more. Mr. Fallon had punched Andy once before, and on another occasion, he'd come awfully close to striking Andy again, shortly after Andy had been shot by Anthony Pearson and had gone out for a brief walk during his recovery at Dr. Nicholas's medical practice. But now, Mr. Fallon reached out benignly, embracing Andy. Dublin immediately felt much better.

Andy, true to his good character, returned the man's hug. He patted Fallon's slender back with genuine warmth. Then he took a step back. Carter Fallon offered his right hand to Andy, a timid and embarrassed smile across his face.

"Friends?" he asked Andy nervously, hoping to confirm that they still were.

"Of course, Carter," Andy replied right away, joyfully and smiling. "For always."

CHAPTER EIGHT

Months passed, and it went from spring to summer to fall, seemingly in the blink of an eye. Andy Caldwell and Carter Fallon had become good friends. Mr. Fallon and Dublin had also grown close. The three of them often spent much time in one another's company.

It was now September, and 1881 was steadily drawing to an impending close. So far, the autumn weather had been pleasant. It was neither too cold nor too warm—not yet, anyhow. And it was frequently sunny.

Dublin had been thoroughly pleased back in July when Marisah's foal, sired by Micah, was born healthy, hardy, and unique. Lakota was the name Dublin gave the little colt that was painted like his sire but the color of his mother. His splashes of color were essentially a replication of Marisah's solid Palomino coloring, and his coat sported large splotches of pure white. Around his right eye was a thick ring of solid black, and that eye was a pretty sky blue like his sire's. His left eye was a deep brown, just like Marisah's. He looked distinctly like a little war pony, so Dublin named him after the Native American tribe of the Northern Plains.

Dublin could hardly wait until it was time to begin assisting Andy and his men with Lakota's training. But that would be a while yet, so he spent a good deal of time with the pretty little horse in an attempt to earn his trust. He eventually gained enough trust so the colt would allow him to place a halter on him and work on his feet. He was able to brush him and comb through his mane and tail, both of which were exceptionally thick, long, and flowing.

Marisah was a good mama. She looked out for her young colt always with watchful eyes. If Dublin happened to work with Lakota beyond his limits and if by chance the colt grew agitated or antsy in any way, Marisah would come charging. It wasn't exactly in an overly aggressive manner, but she would always rush to her foal's side. She often went so far as to shoo Dublin away from Lakota, chasing the teenager away from her baby with her ears pulled back. Dublin would just take off running, usually laughing at her antics. Deep down, though, he did appreciate her valiant devotion to and protection of her colt. Any good mama, horse or human or whatever, would behave in that manner if only to keep her baby from becoming stressed or harmed in any way.

Thoughts and memories of his own mother returned to him in faded, broken pieces, but Dublin determinedly pushed them away from the forefront of his mind. Right now, he didn't want to be reminded of her. Regardless, a painful and familiar tug pulled at the corners of his young heart as he remembered the sweet kindness and benevolence of his mother, the loving, late Destiny Pearson. He recalled her exquisite, lovely, warm face. Then he felt a well-known hollowness in his heart at the thought of his father's lack of care and little to no involvement in Dublin's young life unless it was to chastise him.

Stubbornly, Dublin fiercely shoved all those thoughts to the back of his mind as he continued to work with the colt. He was almost completely successful other than the deep, residual ache that still gripped his heart from countless heartbreaks resulting from his unfit birth father's unloving and harsh actions toward him.

Come on! That was such a long time ago, he told himself.

He glanced up at the sound of horses' hooves upon the hard ground. A smile stretched across his youthful face as he first recognized Seneca approaching him and then even more so once he saw Mr. Fallon riding her. He was happy to take notice that Mr. Fallon appeared to be pleased to have caught sight of Dublin who extended his right hand, waving broadly at him. Fallon promptly returned the wave. He soon was in front of Dublin, mere feet away astride his trusty Appaloosa.

"Howdy, Dublin!" Carter Fallon said, enthusiasm evident in his tone.

The teenager was deeply pleased that his friend was here for a visit. He smiled at the dark-haired man atop the speckled, light-colored horse.

"Hi, Mr. Fallon," Dublin responded, still smiling. "What brings you here today?"

Mr. Fallon shrugged while offering a slight smile. "Oh, nothing really, Dublin. I just wanted some company. Work was light today, and I finished up my last job about an hour ago. And it's only 1:00 in the afternoon. So I thought I'd come and visit my friends."

Dublin nodded. "Well, it is good to see you. Come with me. I think my papa is in the barn right now, fixing up a stall where one of our horses nearly kicked it all the way down."

"Oh, I wish he would have told me. I could have helped him, you know," Carter Fallon said emphatically, dramatically throwing his hands up into the air in an exasperated fashion.

Dublin chuckled, shaking his head slowly from side to side. "No, that's alright. He knew you likely had work to do today. But you could help him now if you like. Let's go!"

Dublin uncharacteristically grasped Mr. Fallon's left wrist with exuberance and began leading him toward the barn where the pounding of a hammer against wooden boards could be heard from inside. Fallon allowed himself to be led in that manner without resisting. He smiled all the way.

Soon they came upon Andy working hard and nailing boards vertically to create a horse stall. The stall had been previously destroyed by a rambunctious, strong horse named Galal. The stallion was currently in another stall while Andy repaired his damaged one.

"Care for me to lend you a hand, Andy?" Carter Fallon asked his friend who was hard at work and hadn't noticed his or his son's presence inside the barn.

Andy, without turning away from his work, nodded slowly and answered him. "Sure, Carter, if you like. Just grab a hold of this board at the top while I nail it right here. Yeah, just like that. Thanks."

Before long, their task was completed, and Galal's stall was not only repaired but also reinforced well in the event the stallion would get a flash of pent-up energy or extreme orneriness and attempt to kick down his stall again.

Andy exhaled forcefully and then looked to his friend with a cheerful smile. "How nice of you to come over to help, just when I was starting to become pretty tired," he commented happily, patting Fallon on the back.

Carter Fallon merely regarded him quietly but with a clearly pleased smile. He was not really all too familiar with being appreciated, even to this day, by Andy and his son. And although it was certainly not unwelcomed, he just struggled at times to accept that Andy had forgiven his admittedly uncalled-for actions prior to their friendship—their friendship that even *he* was surprised had blossomed wondrously despite his shortcomings and prior hostility toward Andy.

Andy was somehow blameless in everything he did in the community. Carter could see that. He attributed it to Andy's being an upright Christian. That was something Carter could not understand, something he couldn't begin to relate to. But one thing was sure, something admirable about Andy Caldwell was that he was kind, humble, and never professed to be perfect. But just how did he do it?

How a man could have faith after a life of hardships and disappointment was beyond Carter, but he longed to have what Andy seemed to possess. Even Andy's son, no more than a young man, seemed to be familiar with the notion of having faith and knowing this God they both devoutly believed in.

But Carter's embittered heart just could not give in to turning toward God, for the Lord seemed constantly absent in his own life. What had made him so defective that God could not shine His light on him, too? Though he longed for peace, love, and completeness, which he'd been lacking, he was resigned to the knowledge that, for him, that sort of life was simply impossible. It would be pointless to cry out to a distant God who had no concern for the miserable likes of him.

Andy regarded Carter, who appeared to be rather deep in thought. The man looked like he was struggling with something in his mind, but Andy chose to leave it to Carter to say anything about it, if he even would. After a few more moments, when it did not appear that the war the man was waging internally was going to be resolved, Andy spoke. He was hoping to divert Fallon's attention to something productive.

"Carter, if you are interested and would like to, I recently noticed a weak board on one side of my barn that is starting to split, and I was going to replace it today. Since you seem eager to help, you're welcome to take a look at it and work your magic on it, if you want to. I mean, I would so appreciate it, for I am fairly exhausted."

Carter readily agreed, nodding even before his friend fully completed his sentence. "Sure, I will help you out and do that for you. Just show me where it is, and I'll get to work right away." He answered with a half smile on his face, his eyes alight with the pleasure of being able to help Andy with more work—work he knew how to do well.

Andy led Carter over to the defective area of the barn with two imperfect boards. Andy had plenty of new wooden boards on hand, so Carter replaced them without difficulty or hesitation. Dublin observed Mr. Fallon working diligently, standing next to his papa and saying not a word while they collaborated on their project. He was impressed and also grateful for the slim man's helpful, willing attitude toward Andy. He had turned out to be a good friend after all.

When Carter finished up, he, Andy, and Dublin gathered up all the surplus supplies and stored them in one of the rooms Andy used for storage for horse supplies and miscellaneous supplies for other repair work.

Carter helped Andy by leading Galal back to his newly repaired stall, and then he secured it shut. The unique Arabian poked his head out of his stall, stretching his neck out so his nose was near Carter's hands, inviting the man to pat him. Carter did so, smiling. The horse snorted after being petted for some time and then wandered over to his feed bucket, munching happily on his grain and oats.

Andy had all his horses in their stalls today. Typically, they would be out to pasture, but he was feeling uncharacteristically exhausted, even for him, so he'd just made certain they had ample amounts of hay and extra oats and grain to sustain them since they wouldn't have access to the grassy pasturelands for grazing. He just couldn't foresee being able to round up all the horses come evening, even with the help of his son, for he had given his hired men the day off. They'd been working extra hours training the younger horses and had even helped out on a few Saturdays. So despite it being Wednesday, Andy offered to give them a break in the middle of the week. He asked them to return to work Thursday and Friday, promising them another day off come Saturday.

> *The horses really ought to be out in the pasture, though,* Andy thought, *so they can move around and graze freely. I shouldn't let being this tired affect my horses' health and happiness.*

"One last thing, Carter. Would you mind helping Dublin and me let the horses out to pasture? I was going to keep them inside the barn for the day to cut back on my work since I'm so tired, but I can't let that stop me from allowing them to enjoy some room to run. Maybe after that I can take a quick nap, and come evening, I'll be refreshed enough to round 'em all back up into the barn on my own."

Carter frowned slightly. "Wonder why you're becoming so tired like you have been, Andy."

Andy merely shrugged it off, feeling slightly annoyed. "Well, I'm not growing any younger. I suppose that's what it is. I'll be alright."

Not looking or feeling entirely convinced but dropping the subject, Carter nodded readily. "Sure, I'll help out with that. Dublin and I can take care of it. Why don't you go inside and rest right now so you can get to feeling better quicker," he said.

"Sounds like a fine idea, Carter. Thank you. You have been a tremendous help to me today. I'm so glad you stopped by. We will have to meet up for a meal sometime soon if we can work it out. Well, anyhow, we'll work it out later on. Take care, my friend. My chair is calling my name," Andy said gratefully with a low chuckle at his last comment.

Carter smiled and nodded, at a loss for words at Andy's praise, but he received it with deep appreciation. Then as Andy ambled toward his farmhouse, Carter locked eyes with Dublin, nodding toward the horses. Dublin nodded, too. They herded all the horses into their pastureland in a fairly timely manner without conversation. But when they finished, Dublin looked up at his former teacher with a grateful smile.

"Thank you for helping us out so much today. I hope you have a good rest of your afternoon, and I look forward to seeing you again soon," Dublin said genuinely.

"My pleasure, Dublin," Fallon said simply, wearing a pleased smile on his face. Once more, it was nice to be so appreciated. But even though he'd had a reasonably decent day, he already knew dejectedly that he was going to go home to have at least a few drinks to pass the time in a numb state rather than be left alone to his merciless, raging thoughts.

Fallon shook the teen's hand, said goodbye, and then walked over to his Appaloosa, swinging into the saddle before setting off down the driveway and heading through town toward his place. His place was always very empty and hopelessly, infuriatingly, deafeningly quiet.

Chapter Nine

D ublin watched as Carter Fallon disappeared from sight, feeling an onslaught of mixed emotions. The man seemed so lonely, like he was searching for something he couldn't quite grasp. Dublin wondered what was holding Mr. Fallon back from reaching for Jesus, for He alone could save him and make a profound and positive difference in his—or anyone's—hurting life.

People of all sorts had burdens that were crushing and weighing down their hearts. They had to deal with the enemy's deceptive lies that told them they were undeserving of love or forgiveness, not to mention enduring years of unimaginable pain and disappointments specific to each person's situations in their own lives.

Pain and a focus on the pain rather than on God—the One who died for all—could distract a man, a woman, or a child from turning to Christ and ultimately being set free from the futility and bondage of sin and this fallen world's dealings.

Then Dublin thought of Andy. His papa was growing so tired more and more frequently, to the point of exhaustion. Sometimes he would nearly collapse. He often went to bed earlier than ever before and would not rise until later than he typically did.

Is it simply stress weighing on him, or is something amiss with his health?

Dublin was fairly certain that if he suggested that Andy see his friend Dr. Nicholas, Andy would decline the suggestion. His papa would totally dismiss the idea that he might need medical intervention.

Feeling rather stressed about his father's well-being, Dublin watched the horses in their pasture for a while. Then he closed the doors to the barn before going inside the farmhouse. In the living room, he discovered Andy looking rather comfortable in his chair, his feet propped up. His snoring was barely audible.

Dublin, who had slept well the previous night, was physically doing quite well and found himself lying down on the sofa before he had a second thought on the matter. Within moments, he was snoozing directly across from his papa.

They both rested for at least half an hour before the two of them were suddenly awakened. The sound of rain could be heard pounding against the tin roof of the old, white farmhouse. It came down in rushing, violent torrents accompanied by powerful, swirling winds from the northeast.

Yawning, Andy stretched luxuriously. He commented to Dublin as he finished yawning and stretching that his nap had been quite welcome but not long enough. Ordinarily, Dublin wouldn't have thought too much about his papa's comment. But now he was in a continuous state of feeling that something was wrong regarding his father's health. He wasn't certain why he was so concerned now, but he wondered if it was because there was some merit to his worry.

Dublin suppressed a yawn and a comment he wanted to say, but he didn't have the bravery to speak up. He decided that maybe he'd allow some more time to pass just to see when or if Andy would get better—or worse. But he wasn't sure that was the best idea, either.

"Well, why don't we go back in the barn and get all the horses' stalls mucked out before we bring the horses in for the evening?" Andy suggested, peering out the window, discovering that the rain had slacked off considerably. "We could make a run for it into the barn and try to avoid getting drenched," he added, a crooked half smile on his handsome face.

Dublin, eager to do something to forget his current troubles, nodded readily. Father and son immediately took off running for the barn as soon as they made it outdoors. Dublin arrived at the barn first, darting inside and escaping the elements under the sturdy shelter. Andy followed mere seconds behind his son, but he was coughing and breathless. Dublin wasn't sure how much longer he could hold his tongue, but he pushed aside the gnawing worry with a forceful mental shove, wordlessly grabbing a shovel. Andy did the same a few minutes later. They worked in stalls next to each other.

Andy's recent slide into unfavorable health was disconcerting to Dublin, and he could tell his papa resented his symptoms. The limitations they brought frustrated him. Regardless, the two of them finished mucking out every stall quickly.

Andy walked outside the barn after the rain sounded as though it had ceased completely. Verifying that it had indeed stopped, he suggested to Dublin that they each catch a horse from the pasture and go for a ride.

"Sure, Papa. That sounds like a fun idea," Dublin responded right away. He was eager to spend time with his father on a leisurely ride. They grabbed some halters and their respective lead ropes, setting out through the wrought-iron gate before wandering over the hill until they came upon the horses they each were hoping to corral.

Dublin wanted to catch Fareed. He'd ridden on the majestic horse on several occasions, so he stood in the pastureland with a patient, quiet, compassionate, and gentle presence before the beautiful stallion. With a lulling voice and his kind demeanor, Dublin was able to quickly work the halter onto the kingly, sooty, buckskin dapple stallion's head. He spoke to the horse soothingly, patting his gracefully arched neck. The regal stallion even went so far as to lean his head against the teenager's cheek. Dublin was delighted.

"Good job, son," Andy said with manifest approval as he was working his halter onto his choice of mounts, Amira, the exotic, vibrant, dark chestnut mare. Despite being a lively example of an Arabian, Amira was relatively calm for Andy.

"Thanks, Papa. Same to you," Dublin responded, smiling a particular smile that endearingly brightened his youthful face.

"Thank you," Andy replied. "Well, let's get these Arabians back into the barn so we can get 'em saddled up before we head on out." Andy patted his son's shoulder while they walked.

Dublin selected Fareed's handsome English saddle and its matching bridle from the tack room, while Andy found Amira's English tack nearby. Then the pair carried their bounty to where their mounts stood tethered, patiently waiting for them.

They worked on tacking up the horses, and when finished, they led their horses outside the barn and into the mild day. A gentle breeze was now blowing about lazily, and the brightly shining sun was peeking through the ever-lightening storm clouds. The clearing sky was now transforming the outdoors into a more pleasant and positive atmosphere.

Might as well take advantage of the nice weather while the daylight is still present, Andy thought, pleased. He felt it was near-perfect outside for a relaxing ride with his son. Andy closed the barn doors behind them. Then they mounted their Arabians and headed toward the southern part of Andy's woods. They began riding alongside each other at a brisk trot.

They crossed a creek and passed by several exquisite caves and rock formations protruding from the hilly ground. They even came across the same herd of deer that Dublin had been able to observe when he'd first come to stay with his papa. It was the herd with the leading piebald buck. To his sheer delight, Dublin noticed that the herd currently included a couple of younger-looking does, both bearing the similar piebald markings. The creatures were so beautiful, including the original, stately buck that had to have been the does' father. Both of the smaller deer had pronounced bright blue eyes rimmed with black, making their piercing eyes more prominent.

Andy glanced over at Dublin and found himself smiling at the look of excitement and pleasure on his son's face. He felt joy in knowing that the pretty sight of this particular herd of deer that knew the Caldwell property as their home turf brought his son such happiness. He and Dublin did not cross paths with this herd of deer frequently, so as always, it was a nice privilege to be able to witness the mysteriously beautiful herbivores, a few of them being unparalleled to the typical whitetail.

"Lord, You never cease to amaze me with all Your beautiful, glorious creation. Thank You for allowing my son and me to see these deer today," Andy murmured softly in reverent praise and awe at the majestic work of God's skilled hands.

Dublin smiled, just barely catching the gist of what Andy had said quietly, praising their God for His beautiful and marvelous craftsmanship in the form of a rare herd of deer.

"Papa, I think it's amazing that God created such beautiful, completely stunning animals like these deer. He has such creativity and a perfect imagination, one I could never hope to imitate. The Lord certainly has unfathomable and limitless ideas and skill. How do you think He thought up this whole world and all that goes on—from nothing?"

Andy glanced over at his son while they rode onward, bearing a smile on his handsome face. "Well, Dublin, that is a very good question. I don't know the answer, to be honest. But we don't need to worry about all the hows and the whys. I imagine that once we all make it to heaven, God might share His reasons for why and how with us as we sit peacefully at His feet. In the meantime, perhaps it might be a good idea to just appreciate and give Him praise for all His hard work, His creativity, and perhaps most of all, the fact that He cares so much for us, for He is so lovingly involved in our lives.

"I love giving Him praise for His supreme plans for our individual lives, His working them out for the better, teaching us and helping us grow in faith and ultimately grow closer to Him. Sometimes, though, it can be uncomfortable or painful for us along the journey."

Dublin's eyes searchingly met Andy's as they rode along side by side at a slow pace. Then he replied, "I do not understand still to this day why my life had to start out the way it did. But I will say that I'm somehow grateful that it did so it would all lead up to where I'd meet you and be adopted by you, a father who actually loves me and wants me—and to get to a point where I could finally meet Jesus. It feels a tad bit strange to say it like that, but it's true. I can praise Him for my biological family's bad situation and especially for it ultimately leading me toward something better. For it all led up to a relationship with Him."

Taken aback by his son's admission regarding his past, Andy smiled. His perspective was certainly positive. And it was true. His boy was growing up right. Dublin had already matured into a very good young man with such potential. Andy took great pride in his son. He would overcome. Of this, Andy was certain.

Thanks be to God, Andy prayed silently, *that Dublin feels like he belongs somewhere now and feels loved and safe. Also, I thank You that he is so sensitive and compassionate, a tenderhearted young man filled with love and respect for others. He so easily could have turned into someone else with opposing qualities as a direct result of his upbringing. Lord, You are to be praised for my son's bright and hopeful future and for his happy life now that he's always deserved.*

"Bless you, my son," said Andy aloud. "That's a mature take on what happened to you throughout your life. I am incredibly proud of you." Dublin regarded him silently and maybe a bit awkwardly. But then the teenager wore a clear look of determination and pleasure on his face, along with an encouraged smile on his lips.

They continued along slowly until they were met with more rainy weather. Soon the clouds grew dark again. Thankfully, though, the rain was only barely falling from the sky. It was no more than a very light shower. So Andy and Dublin turned their horses around and started back toward home before the rain had a chance to intensify.

When they made it back to the Caldwell property, the rain had actually let up to an even gentler sprinkling over the land. With tired-looking eyes and slower movements than usual, Andy suggested that he and Dublin go ahead and bring their herd of horses inside the barn before it became dark out, or before Andy ran out of steam.

Dublin offered to herd all the horses from the pasture into the barn and into their individual stalls on his own while Andy took care of their riding horses, removed their tack, brushed them down, and made sure they had ample food and water.

Once they accomplished both of their respective tasks and each horse was secured and content in their own stalls, Andy and Dublin, both weary, made their way into the farmhouse. Andy was exhausted, but he set to heating up some dinner for him and his boy anyway. Dublin immediately assisted him, saying nothing although his mind raged with worrisome thoughts about his papa and the man's newfound lack of endurance.

They prayed and then ate their dinner without much conversation. Dublin looked at his papa, perturbed, as Andy told him that he was afraid he was going to have to turn in for the night. It was only 6:00 in the evening.

An onslaught of emotions welled up in Dublin, and he suddenly became aware of tears threatening to spill from his intensely deep-blue eyes. But before they could fall freely, he willed them back and turned his head to the right so his father might be unmindful of his strong emotions. However, Dublin was not able to mask his worry with enough discretion.

Andy reached out and placed his large hands gently on Dublin's shoulders as he stood in front of him. Then he touched his son's left cheek. In doing so, he simultaneously brushed away a lone tear that had overflowed from Dublin's shining eye.

"Son, I know you are worried about me. It tears me up inside to see you worry about me and see your obvious pain because of it. If it will help ease your concern, I will take a ride into town tomorrow and see Jacob, if he has the time. I have been trying to ignore how I've been feeling, but clearly, something isn't quite right with me. I'm sorry you're going through such turmoil because of my health. I'm seeing that the best thing I can do for myself and for you, my son, is to take better care of myself. I love you, Dublin, and it is my prayer that I will be well enough to be here for a very long time."

Dublin stared into his papa's kindly brown eyes. He could see the fear in those dark eyes. Pure fear masked the strength and confidence that typically resided in them.

"Dublin, I won't sit here and tell you that all will be fine with me, but we just need to put our trust in the One who holds our futures. God is still in control, so let's just pray that my ailments will resolve in time. But no matter what, God loves us, and He won't ever abandon us. Try not to worry, son. Remember, none of us is guaranteed tomorrow, so we need to take each day as it comes and be thankful for that gift."

Dublin opened his mouth as though to speak, but he couldn't say a word. Rising emotions still intensely clogged his throat. Pulling him close, Andy hugged him. Dublin buried his face against his papa's chest. Tears stung at his eyes and trailed slowly down his cheeks, wetting the front of Andy's shirt. Andy paid no heed to the sudden dampness as he held his son tightly. But Andy could not fight the moisture that gathered in his own eyes as he pondered what his ailment could potentially mean for their futures.

CHAPTER TEN

Dublin remained awake late into the night, even though Andy had retired to bed at 6:30. Dublin sat in the living room, solemn and feeling like he was losing his sanity. He read his Bible by firelight until well past dusk. Then he simply sat, his legs curled up on the sofa and off to one side, lost in his thoughts.

Occasionally, Dublin lifted up his concerns to the Lord in prayer, baring his soul of all his fears and many uncertainties that were barraging his young heart. Eventually, he glanced toward the grandfather clock, discovering with a start that it was nearing midnight. He abruptly rose from the sofa before he put out the fire, which had been gradually dying down for the past hour and a half. Walking up the stairs slowly, he stifled a broad yawn. As he walked past Andy's bedroom, he could hear his father breathing steadily, snoring. That gave him the reassurance he needed that Andy was, for now, doing alright.

Dublin peeled off his shirt and then removed his boots before crawling wearily into his bed. He lay down, pulling the sheet up along with a light blanket. He snuggled comfortably, surrounded by warmth and the soft, cozy texture of the blanket.

As he lay there, Dublin's thoughts were many. *How blessed by God am I that in addition to my loving papa, I have a warm and comfortable bed, a nice house, nice clothes, my own horses , and everything else I need. To think that I have not always had basic necessities provided for me astounds me to this day, that my biological father never felt it necessary to make certain I had fitting clothes, shoes, or enough food. I am awed that Andy would go without to ensure that I have all I need. What a drastic difference between two adult men! How is it possible that the man who actually fathered me also hated me, while a complete stranger saved me from my father and then became my father?*

That father has shown me love, acceptance, and protection. He's provided for all my needs and has been supportive of me, showing me a gentleness I haven't known since my mama was here on this earth with me. Dear Lord, please be with my papa and heal him of anything that's wrong with him. I know You hold the power to heal him and give him the strength and wellness he needs. You know, Father God, how much I need him. Your will be done. In Jesus's name. Amen.

Dublin continued to lie there wide awake despite the fact that he was so fatigued physically and emotionally. His pondering of the uncertainties ahead of him and his father wearied him, yet were seemingly unstoppable.

Rain tapped against the roof rhythmically, calming Dublin's heart. Even so, sleep evaded him. Eventually, he fell asleep, succumbing to utter exhaustion sometime after 2:00 in the morning.

Predictably, the next morning came a bit too soon. He'd simply stayed awake too long into the night, and it hadn't helped any that most of it was accompanied by anxiety. But he'd awakened in a good frame of mind. His dreams had been harmless and hopeful in nature. He said a quick, silent prayer of thanksgiving to God for waking him up and allowing him yet another night void of any nightmares. It was becoming more and more of a nightly routine to have pleasant dreams. It was certainly an improvement from three years ago. He welcomed the respite.

Dublin knew he owed his thanks to God. He believed that the Lord was steadily continuing to offer him healing from his heartbreaking, horrific past. Promptly rolling out of bed, Dublin sprang to his feet. He selected from his closet a clean, blue, lightweight, long-sleeved shirt. Pulling it over his head, he exchanged the socks on his feet for a fresh pair and then laced up his work boots. Glancing in his mirror, he took his comb and ran it through his short, wavy hair in an attempt to make it appear more presentable.

At his age, he had been shaving his facial hair for about a year and a half now. He could see today that his face could stand to be shaved, for he had plenty of stubble. He generally did not mind doing it, but this morning he was slightly annoyed by having to take the time. He was chomping at the bit to see his papa, to see how he was faring.

Once he finished, he took a towel, and wiping his face, he peered into his mirror again and offered a pleased smile toward his reflection. Dublin then gazed into the mirror for several more moments, taking in his more mature look that had seemed to appear only recently. He was somehow looking quite grown-up.

And he looked very much like Anthony Pearson. Dublin surmised that he probably looked nearly identical to his biological father when he was a younger man—all but his eyes that were reminiscent of his mother's beautiful blue ones. Knowing he had many of Anthony's facial features was not comforting to Dublin, not so much because he believed he was unattractive but because it was unsettling to him that he closely resembled a man who'd scarred him in many ways. He was a man who had scarred him to the point where he would somehow always be affected by the man's rigid absence of love.

Dublin knew he ought to forgive Anthony entirely, once and for all, and let go of the remaining resentment he held for the dead man. For what good would come of his holding on to his ill will toward his deceased biological father? Deep down, he knew the residual hatred and bitter resentment bound him in a way that would weigh on his heart and mind until he would be able to fully release it. He just needed to trust God regarding the matter.

Maybe someday he'd be able to, but he was simply unable to forgive that man for all he had done to him while he was alive. More importantly, it was hard to let go of all that Anthony hadn't done. It seemed an insurmountable feat, but he recalled Jesus's words from scripture that with God, all things are possible.

He left it at that for the time being. Dublin was hopeful that the Lord would someday help him forgive the unforgivable in Anthony Pearson. The wrongs committed against him were in a time past, a past that wouldn't reoccur now or ever again. He felt lighter and a little braver than he did moments ago.

Looking outside his bedroom window, Dublin saw that the September sun was shining brightly, making for an autumn morning that was both pleasant and energizing. It was thankfully far from a dreary day.

He stepped outside his room, noticing that Andy had already risen. Relieved that he wasn't still sleeping from the fatigue that plagued him without mercy, Dublin smiled to himself. He started down the stairs, making his way into the kitchen. Andy was already finished making breakfast and was placing his and Dublin's plates on the table when Dublin came through the doorway. Andy looked up, appearing remarkably bright-eyed, and he smiled as his son joined him for breakfast.

"Hi, son. How're you this fine morning?" Andy asked, patting Dublin's shoulder.

Dublin returned his father's smile and nodded. "Well, I am doing fine, just a little sleepy. I was up late last night. But never mind about that. I will be alright. I'm just happy to see you looking this rested for the first time in a long while," he responded, his final sentence more of an exuberant exclamation.

Andy was sympathetic to his son's tiredness from being up late. However, he merely suggested that they eat their breakfast for some needed energy for the day before they began their work with the horses. Dublin was grateful that Andy did not ask him why he was awake so late. He was also glad he'd avoided expressing a bunch of sympathetic remarks about Dublin's being tired. He didn't want his papa to make a big fuss over his condition when it was Andy's condition that needed more attention.

Dublin silently gave thanks to God for the apparent improvement in his father's appearance. They sat down, and Andy offered up thanksgiving for their food and for the new day. He also prayed for good health for him and Dublin, expressing his thanks for the fact that today he felt significantly better. He closed the prayer, and they both looked up. Their gazes met, joyful smiles spreading across both their lips simultaneously.

"Papa, are you still going to go see Dr. Nicholas sometime today? I am incredibly relieved that you do feel and seem so much better, but I hope...I hope you will still go see him. I want to be sure you don't need any doctoring for what's been going on with you..." Dublin's voice trailed off as he grew worried—worried once more that Andy's unknown illness might soon return with an awful vengeance.

Andy smiled as he picked up his fork and took a bite of his breakfast before he answered. "Well, I figure I ought to. So yes, I will ride into town and see him. I think I'll do it this afternoon. That way I can at least get some work done around here first."

Dublin hesitated for a brief moment. "Do you mind if I go with you?"

"No, not at all. In fact, I would like for you to come with me. And Jake would love to see you, especially since you're doing well. I know he doesn't enjoy seeing you hurt or sick, son. He only wants for you to be healthy." He paused. "Of course, he probably won't like having to examine me for some ailment, either. But I guess since that is his job, he'll have to be alright with it. Isn't that right?"

Dublin offered a half smile and nodded in solemn agreement with Andy. They finished eating their breakfast in quiet, companionable silence. Dublin washed the dishes as Andy dried them and put them back in their usual places where they were kept when not in use.

Walking together outside and into the pleasantly warm, lazy, breezy morning, father and son made their way to the barn and worked together to herd their horses out to the pasture. Then they did their usual morning routine of mucking the stalls and filling up the feed and water buckets in every stall.

Les and the men all arrived shortly after Andy and Dublin finished their chores. They all collaborated as a team to decide what to do for the day. The men were to work mainly with Kamaria since she was coming along well in her training. Akilah was healing from a sprain in her left hind leg. Andy was waiting for that to heal completely before working with her again so as not to cause further injury and unnecessary pain for the filly.

Andy worked with his men while Dublin observed and occasionally helped out. Andy allowed Les to make decisions in much of the training methods. But Andy found that he was beginning to grow tired come lunchtime. He realized all at once that he felt poorly.

Dublin fixed him and his papa some lunch and then encouraged Andy that now was probably a good time to see Dr. Nicholas. Andy nodded wordlessly, and after they cleaned up their lunch dishes, they set to saddling and bridling their horses. Mounting up, they soon started off toward town.

They rode at a laid-back trot, riding without conversation all the way into London and over to Dr. Jacob Nicholas's practice. They dismounted, both tying their horses to the hitching post provided, and walked side by side into the medical office.

Jacob didn't have any patients right then, but he was seated at his desk appearing rather busy with his notes. He glanced up, his kindly light brown eyes alight with pleasure as soon as he recognized two of his best friends.

"Hi there, Andy and Dublin," he said in a booming voice, rising to shake Andy's hand and then to pat Dublin robustly on the shoulder. "What has brought you Caldwells here today? Wait a minute. Are you two doing alright?" Jacob regarded them worriedly.

"Well," Andy drawled hesitantly, "I'm not sure. Thankfully, Dublin here is doing quite well. I…I have actually come here for, uh, myself. I was wondering if you could take a few moments and do some sort of examination on me, Jake. You see, Jacob, I haven't been feeling well lately. I've been awfully tired most of the time, more like exhausted really. I have noticed that I get out of breath much easier than I used to, and I've lost much of my strength, too."

Jacob's lips pursed, a pronounced look of concern crossing his handsome features. He motioned for Andy and Dublin to follow him into a room. He directed Andy to have a seat on a cot. He immediately took a stethoscope and began listening to Andy's heart. He listened for what seemed like a very long time. Then the doctor asked Andy to remove his boots and socks. Confused but willing to comply, Andy did just that. Dr. Nicholas knelt down and rolled up both of Andy's pant legs, examining his ankles. Dublin thought they looked swollen. A gnawing fear began to eat at him ravenously.

After the doctor finished his examination, taking into consideration Andy's recollection of his symptoms, he made both a frightening and heartbreaking announcement about what he believed was wrong with Andy.

"Andy, I'm afraid that it seems you have heart failure," Jacob said. The pain in his voice was evident as he spoke haltingly. But he was very certain of his diagnosis for his dear friend.

Dublin felt a stab of pain deep within his own chest as he listened to the doctor's harsh identification of what was wrong with his beloved father.

No, Lord, Dublin cried out silently. *This can't be! Andy can't have heart failure. I can't lose him. Please, Father, don't let this be true.*

But as Dr. Nicholas explained with confidence the common symptoms of the illness and what he'd observed during his examination, Dublin knew. He knew with a dark sense of dread that the doctor had diagnosed Andy appropriately. The prognosis was typically not very hopeful, Dr. Nicholas shared with the newly diagnosed, very ill man and his very scared boy.

"But," Jacob continued, struggling to keep his emotions at bay and remain professional, "there *is* a treatment available. I can give you specific, small doses of foxglove extract known as digitalis, which might actually work really quite well and for a long time. We won't know until we try, Andy, but I do recommend that you try this plant's extract as a remedy for your heart failure."

Andy just sat there on the cot taking in both the devastating and also semihopeful information that had just been thrown at him in no more than a few brief moments. He felt a lump in his throat form, not so much out of self-pity or fear that he might die soon, but for his son. The boy still needed him, he felt, and Andy was frightened that if he passed away, Dublin wouldn't cope well after losing him. And Andy had waited a long time to be blessed with Dublin as his son. He didn't want the wonderful, tender memories to end for him or for the teenager.

Lord, help us, Andy cried out in his heart. *Please be with us and give us Your strength and mercy, and bless us with abundant time together, regardless of my prognosis.*

Please, for my son's sake, Lord.

CHAPTER ELEVEN

The medicinal extract from the foxglove plant seemed to influence Andy's health overall in a positive manner in barely over a week's time. Andy could tell his heart was functioning more effectively since he was able to do more without becoming quite so out of breath. His energy level was better, too. Even the swelling in his ankles had diminished considerably.

He was filled with joy and praised God for His mercy in allowing the otherwise poisonous biennial plant's healing components to work inside his body and so well. He truly thanked the Lord for giving him more time on earth with his precious son, his strong son.

Andy decided that he and Dublin ought to spend the day with Carter Fallon. It had been a long while since Carter had stopped by for a visit with them, and Andy found that he dearly missed his company.

It was Saturday, and Andy didn't have Les and the other men working for him today or the next. The horses had already been let out to pasture. It was a pleasant, sunny day, and the temperature was warm. Though the ground was muddy in many places, still damp and soft, the ample sunshine was more than enough to create in Andy a happy, lighthearted, and contented attitude.

Dublin was working with his little Paint colt, Lakota. When he finished up with him, he started toward the barn to try to track down his father. He found Andy busily tacking up Midnight with Marguerite tethered nearby, already fully saddled and bridled.

"Where are we going, Papa?" Dublin asked him.

Andy looked up from his task at hand. "Well, I thought we might ride on over to Mr. Fallon's place for a visit. It's been a while since he's been over here, and we haven't come across him at all in town lately. So I just thought it would be nice for us to surprise him at his home. What do you say, son?"

"Sure, Papa. I'd like that very much," Dublin replied immediately. His heart warmed at the pleasant thought of visiting a good friend. "Oh, and thank you for saddling up Marguerite. Are you feeling alright?"

Andy nodded emphatically as he tightened the girth on his old horse for the final time. A big smile lit up his face. "Sure thing, son. That medicine has drastically improved my stamina and overall feeling of well-being. I feel so much better than I have for some time now. Well. Are you ready to go?"

"I'm glad, and very relieved, Papa. Oh, and yes, I am ready. Let's go." Dublin's voice was filled with excitement, and he had a bright, eager smile on his face.

Dublin and Andy mounted their horses. Soon they were heading in the direction of the home that belonged to Carter Fallon, located just east of London. It was a bit of a long trip, for the Caldwells lived to the west of the Ohio town, but Andy and Dublin enjoyed every moment of their journey together. As they neared their friend's home, they anticipated meeting up with him for an enjoyable visit. They hadn't gone over to Fallon's home often. In fact, they had only been there two or three times to see him before today.

His home was a bit run down, but Andy and Dublin were blind to the disrepair as well as the clutter. They simply enjoyed being able to see their friend and spend time with him. They tethered their mounts to a hitching post that Carter had built years ago underneath a lean-to shelter for potential visitors' horses. The shelter was underneath a shady maple tree, making it quite comfortable for horses to stand under and patiently wait on their riders until the time came to depart.

Carter Fallon had buckets intended for water and oats available in the lean-to for any visiting horses' potential hunger and thirst while they stood waiting, but he did not keep them full. He typically had no company, not frequently anyhow. So Andy and Dublin needed to see if Carter would spare some horse feed and the use of his springhouse to water their horses if they were to stay long.

Andy knocked on the front door and waited for his friend to come to the door and greet them. Dublin stood just slightly behind Andy. They waited several long moments, but Fallon didn't open the door. Worried, Andy knocked on the door again, more sharply this time, and waited once more. Finally, the door opened, and Carter Fallon, looking haggard, appeared in the doorway.

"Hey, Andy. Hey, Dublin," he said, perceptibly slurring his words. At once, Dublin bristled instinctively. He could tell that his former teacher was intoxicated. The slender man's gray eyes were bloodshot, and his expression was what one might call glazed over. His breath smelled of liquor.

Even though the handyman didn't seem angry or short-tempered, Dublin did not like being around him when he was like this. Truthfully, more than anything else at the moment, he wanted to run back to his horse. Mr. Fallon's easygoing manner could morph easily into something else, but then again, maybe not. Regardless, Dublin felt uncomfortable in his presence since he was fully aware that Mr. Fallon wasn't totally in control of himself. The man could potentially be unpredictable—dangerous.

Andy, too, recognized that Fallon was intoxicated. Protectively, he stood directly in front of Dublin, acting as a shield if need be. He wanted to give the young man a sense of safety, knowing fully how this must be affecting him.

"Hey, Carter. Are you feeling alright, my friend?" Andy asked.

"Yeah, you bet," Carter slurred, wavering as he stood. "Here. Why don't you boys come on in? Hey. Sorry I haven't been around in a while. Things haven't been too great around here, and I haven't felt like venturing out to too many places."

Andy frowned, feeling concerned about his friend. When he was able to decipher exactly what the man was trying to tell him, he finally spoke, troubled, asking, "Why, Carter? What's going on?"

Carter didn't reply. Instead, he stared at Andy without any identifiable expression on his face for several seconds. Suddenly, he motioned for Andy and Dublin to come into his house. He stumbled back into his home, his visitors following behind with caution. The house was in utter disarray. There were empty bottles of beer and other alcoholic beverages scattered all over the wooden floor in the living room and littering the entire sitting surface of the sofa. Trash and personal belongings were also scattered across the floor and on the other pieces of furniture. Plates of half-eaten food were piled up on a couple of Carter's end tables and on one of the shelves on his bookshelf.

Andy's heart hurt greatly for Carter and his obvious struggles. While he knew some of his friend's past, it seemed as though something was going on presently to have made him overindulge and neglect keeping his living space clean.

Carter gestured for Andy and Dublin to take a seat in two of the chairs in the living room, the ones not covered in any bottles, trash, or anything else. They both settled into their respective seats. Dublin sat rigidly, apprehensive by the littered, disorderly environment and by Mr. Fallon's evident drunkenness. But he chose to bravely remain indoors even though his flight instincts wanted to fully take over.

Dublin was unwilling to appear rude by striding right back out the door without explanation. He believed, at least partially, that his papa would be able to protect him if Carter Fallon should lose control and potentially attempt to attack him in some manner. His heart hurt at the thought of his friend doing such a thing, and it also pained him that the man was obviously in pain himself. Saying a silent prayer that Mr. Fallon would remain civil, Dublin sat in his chair, not moving, save for his controlled breathing in and out.

"I got fired from my repair job," Carter slurred suddenly. He stopped speaking just as abruptly, giving no further detail and showing no apparent emotion. In fact, he seemed overly nonchalant about a significant misfortune in his life.

"Oh, Carter," Andy cried out, now even more concerned for his friend. "I'm so terribly sorry! What happened, my friend?"

Fallon could hardly look straight at Andy Caldwell. His head was bobbing slightly as he tried to focus his gaze on his friend. But because his world was spinning relentlessly, he didn't succeed.

"Well," he drawled loudly, looking away, "there was a man I was doing work for, and he kept insulting me. And then he got in my face, so I pushed him away from me. He punched me, and then I punched him in return. I might have…I might have beaten that sorry big shot into a pulp 'fore it was said and done, and therefore, I was fired. Fired! Again!"

Fallon paused. Then he added rather heatedly, "Just like you had me fired from my job before this one!"

Carter Fallon essentially roared his last sentence. And even though he had been calm in the moments prior, he was growing increasingly agitated. Andy hurriedly directed Dublin to go outside for the teenager's physical safety. Andy would remain inside to try to reason with his intoxicated friend. But somewhere from within, he suspected that reasoning with Carter was going to be an impossible feat. Even so, he tried.

"Now, Carter, you know you deserved to be let go of your teaching position. Yes, it *was* my doing that you were fired, but you messed up. I'm sorry it came to that, but, Carter, that is all in the past. You have already since owned up to having made that mistake. You've apologized, too, so why get angry at me all over again? We're friends now, aren't we?"

Dublin made his way outdoors, precariously stepping quickly over all the scattered trash that was strewn all over the floor. Now he was outside, but he felt a rising apprehension at leaving his papa inside alone with Carter Fallon.

Mr. Fallon now stood before Andy, enraged. Dublin remained directly outside Mr. Fallon's closed front door, fearing that Andy was going to be assaulted. With the way Mr. Fallon's voice kept intensifying in force and volume each time he responded to Andy's pleas and reasoning, Dublin wasn't certain precisely what was in store for his father.

Andy continued trying to break through to Carter Fallon, but to no avail. Carter was hopelessly drunk and growing more and more riled with each second that passed. His short temper and current altered state of mind weren't a good combination. He lunged toward Andy attempting to tackle him to the filthy, cluttered floor. Andy sidestepped and resisted once Fallon made contact. Due to Fallon's aggression and persistence, though, Andy ended up on the floor anyway. Fallon stood back up, towering over Andy who was trying to convey a nonthreatening attitude on his part.

Andy refused to retaliate; instead, he continued to speak to his drunken friend in a firm yet kind manner. Then he finally realized the futility in attempting to reason with the drunk, angry, spiteful man.

"Now, Carter, I don't know if you'll remember these words, but while I still desire to be your friend, I am going to have to leave. Your behavior, it's—it's ridiculous. Rather than one of us saying—or doing—something we won't be able to take back, I'm out of here, right now."

Then Andy paused, heartsick. His voice softened. "Please, Fallon. Take care of yourself. Try to start easing up on all your drinking. It's not helping your situation any. So I will see you again, perhaps, if you decide for yourself to come see me as friends. Alright? If you need anything, I will try to help you out, my friend."

Carter Fallon responded by scowling and then looking about for a suitably large enough bottle to hurl at Andy Caldwell in order to shut him up and get him out of his house.

Andy sensed that Fallon still wasn't amicable toward him, and by the looks of the man's body language, he figured he'd better get going. So he picked himself up from off the floor, brushed off his clothes, turned, and headed for the door.

Carter sneered at Andy's turned back and promptly hurled an empty liquor bottle at him. The bottle hit its target with a mighty force. Andy flinched, ignoring the pain the abrupt impact had caused. He opened the front door, leaving Fallon alone with his dominating, self-destructive behaviors. Stepping outside, Andy gently closed the door behind him, even though he felt like slamming it shut in frustration—in anger even.

CHAPTER TWELVE

"Papa! What happened? Are you alright?" Dublin asked. Andy broodingly walked right past his son and toward their tethered horses, not saying a word.

Then Dublin flinched and ducked in fright when he heard the sound of shattering glass and something else crashing to the floor inside Carter Fallon's home. Jogging to catch up to his papa, he was inwardly worried about Mr. Fallon but even more worried about his father. He questioned Andy again about whether he was alright.

As they untied their mounts, Andy finally met his son's gaze. Dublin noticed a look of raw pain clouding his father's chocolaty-brown eyes.

"I'm fine, son," he responded, a lump lodged in his throat. "But as for Mr. Fallon, the man is a disaster. As you saw, he'd been self-medicating with alcohol—lots of it. He was so hopelessly drunk today, obstinate, uncaring, aggressive. You know how a person can get when they're drunk. Anyhow, he told me he recently lost his job as the town's handyman. He was angry after being insulted and struck by a man at a work site. Carter told me he punched him and then ended up beating him before it was all over.

"Then he brought up how I'd cost him his job when he was a school teacher around here. I tried to reason with him, but it was no use. He tried to tackle me to the floor, and I lost my balance and fell. When I got up to leave, he threw an empty bottle at me, and it hit me. I guess even though his behavior is self-destructive, he needs to be alone, no company. My being there surely did not do a bit of good."

Andy paused. "He's in no state to be alone, though. He needs a friend. I…I just can't do it. I want to be his friend, but right now he won't hear of it. And I won't put your safety or mine on the line to try to reason with him while he's acting out of his mind. I don't know that it would do any good."

"Are you sure you aren't hurt, Papa?" Dublin asked insistently, concerned.

Andy nodded affirmatively, looking away. They climbed onto their horses and rode safely away from the ill-tempered man's property toward home. As they rode, Dublin, shaken up by Fallon's behavior, suddenly thought of something that downright frightened him deep down to the core of his being.

"Papa, that Harvey Adamson, he isn't going to be let out of jail anytime soon, is he? He's already been locked up for five months, and I don't know what Sheriff Walters's idea of a 'long while' is for keeping that evil man contained." Dublin's ever-deepening voice trailed off. He felt nervous and uncertain.

Andy glanced over at his son and then smiled warmly. "No, son, he isn't. I actually crossed paths with Sheriff Walters the other day, and he assured me that Adamson will be locked up indefinitely. Walters has him in a very secure cell. He isn't going anywhere, Dublin. Don't trouble yourself about it a moment longer, son," Andy said reassuringly.

Dublin released a long, slow exhale of relief. Feeling placated for the moment, Dublin began thinking about Samuel Geoffreys, his best friend since his arrival in London, Ohio. He hadn't allowed himself to think about Samuel in a long time due to the pain that resulted from thinking of him. Sam and his family had packed up a year ago in the spring and moved out West. He missed his friend badly.

Sam had been an intensely bright and welcoming presence on his first day of school in London when he first came to live with Andy. Sam was energetic, rambunctious, adventurous, and incredibly loyal. He was a true and most faithful friend. Dublin truly missed him. Samuel and his family now lived somewhere in Deer Lodge, Montana Territory. Occasionally, the boys would write to each other, but that wasn't the same as spending time with each other face-to-face.

As Dublin and Andy continued to ride toward home, Dublin suddenly made a connection he hadn't made before. His biological father's brother, his uncle, Jimmy Pearson, also lived somewhere in Montana Territory. After Anthony Pearson died, Dublin's memory nearly erased completely any recollections of Uncle Jimmy. After all, Dublin had since and even prior to Anthony's death looked to Andy Caldwell as his rightful, loving father.

Dublin never realized that his best friend and his biological father's brother potentially resided in the same region. He had never met his uncle, though. Jimmy was Anthony's older brother. Dublin still hoped to meet him one day, provided his uncle was even still alive and well. Perhaps someday he might be able to travel to Montana Territory to visit both Samuel and Jimmy Pearson.

Dublin was fairly certain he'd never be able to make the journey all that way to reunite with his best buddy in the world or be successful in finding his uncle. He and Andy simply had far too many responsibilities on the horse farm, probably until forever, to break away and take months or likely longer off for a trip and then return home after the visit. Knowing this brought down his spirits, but before he knew it, he and Andy had ridden all the way back to their horse farm.

After putting the horses out to pasture, Andy and Dublin sought out the hired men who were just finishing up a day's training with Kamaria. The little horse had reached her limitations for the day, but she'd done well. Andy dismissed his employees for the remainder of the day. He was pleased with what Les told him about the filly's quick progress.

Father and son then prepared their dinner, ate together, and cleaned up their dishes and counter surfaces in their cozy kitchen. Then they decided to study the Bible together for a while. Andy led the study, focusing on the book of Romans. While Andy read the entire eighth chapter, Dublin eagerly absorbed verse 18 deep within his heart and soul. "For I reckon that the sufferings of this present time are not worthy to be compared with the glory which shall be revealed in us."

He held on to the hope that one day all his sufferings in this life would cease, that someday all his pain would be worth living through and forgotten forever. His faith in Jesus was strong. And although sometimes that faith wavered from doubt and fear, it always seemed as though the Lord drew him gently but securely back to His side.

In Dublin's past experiences with doubt or any form of shortcoming, God always brushed him off after setting him back on his feet, always on solid ground and on the path of the truth. With the Lord's steady and loving guidance, Dublin was certain his intense fears and the relentless, ruminating thoughts that rolled through his mind continuously would one day be more easily controlled.

God would never abandon him, nor would He ever stop working in him. He was loved so much by the Lord, even when he couldn't feel it. God loved Dublin—even his scars, fears, tears, hurts, and everything else—enough to send Jesus to die for him and for all who might call on Him for forgiveness and salvation. Jesus's death enabled Dublin to have eternal life, ever-present peace, and reconciliation with God the Father.

By Jesus's willing, humble, and loving sacrifice, God also gave Dublin the Holy Spirit who would forever bear witness that Dublin was, indeed, permanently a child of God. So why would Dublin continue to allow fear to corrupt his God-given peacefulness when God had already done such incredible things for him, when He'd already given him so many wonderful, life-changing gifts? Dublin had to admit, though, that he felt rather guilty that he couldn't repay the magnitude of God's blessings that He'd lavishly given him already. He shared his thoughts with Andy.

"Thank you for another thought-provoking Bible study, Papa. I'm learning much with you. Whenever we study the Bible, I keep recognizing what I need to do on my part to change, to be more like Christ, and then to let God do His work in me. Thank you, for caring enough to teach me, even on the days I do not understand much about the scriptures."

Andy offered him a bright smile, feeling the joy overflow within his heart. It was wonderful how his only son was learning and steadily maturing right before his eyes.

"Why, you're welcome, son. I love spending time with you in the Word. You are certainly an intelligent pupil, and you're very sensitive to the Holy Spirit. And remember that though we are saved, we all will still struggle with fleshly troubles such as fear, pain, and temptation. The list goes on and on.

"But through the Spirit in us, we are able to live spiritually. We're strengthened against the distractions and temptations of this fallen world. We can and always will continue to grow, becoming more like Christ Himself. That's what God wants for us. I can tell that you, son, have a soft, pliable heart. You desperately desire to be who God wants you to be. You're doing just fine, Dublin. Just remember that."

Dublin smiled confidently at his father's loving and reassuring comment, contemplating all that Andy had said to him. Shortly after, they ventured outside, corralling all the horses into their respective stalls and seeing to all their needs for the evening. Dublin suggested to his father that they take a leisurely walk after finishing their chores.

As they were walking among the dense woodlands, Dublin suddenly reached around and hugged Andy exuberantly with his left arm. Andy flinched slightly. Concerned, Dublin was curious to inspect his father's injury, recalling that he'd been struck by Mr. Fallon who'd hurled a glass bottle at him. He wanted to make sure the injury wasn't too serious. He certainly didn't want to take any more chances with his papa's health.

Dublin lifted up the back of Andy's shirt and took a look at his back. Raising his shirt had scraped and exposed a large, darkening bruise at the center of his lower back. It was nothing more than a bruise, but Dublin was rather deeply chagrined that he may have just aggravated his papa's undeserved injury from earlier in the day.

"Papa, that looks rather painful. I…I'm so sorry I hurt you."

Andy thought Dublin sounded awfully bothered over the matter. *He* certainly wasn't. But it was sweet of his son to show concern for him. He smiled at that thought.

"No worries at all, son," he replied. "It is sore, but I'm sure it will heal just fine before long."

Andy paused, observing inwardly how tenderhearted his son truly was. And while Dublin's careful concern for him was incredibly heartwarming, the boy's desperate aversion to causing him additional pain was sobering. He sought to reassure his anxious son.

"Oh, and you didn't hurt me any worse. The bruise that is surely there is simply tender, and I reacted instinctively. I'm truly fine. Please do not worry about me, Dublin. Come now, son. Fallon didn't hurt me that bad," he added, winking mischievously. Then he felt intensely regretful that he'd made a joke at Carter's expense.

Forgive me, Lord.

Dublin smiled, about halfway placated and halfway unconvinced. "All right, well, that's good," he replied, distracted by his wandering thoughts.

The two of them continued on their walk for another mile before they turned and headed home. It was now at the beginning stage of dusk. When they got home from their walk, Andy drew a bath, first for Dublin and then for himself. Each took turns enjoying a relaxing and refreshing bath after a long and trying day.

After they were both finished, they found their usual spots for further relaxation, Andy in his chair and Dublin sprawled out on his sofa. Dublin glanced over at his papa who had already succumbed to sleeping in his chair. His breathing had slowed and was even. He looked to be sleeping restfully. Smiling, Dublin recounted his many blessings in a silent prayer offered up to God from his heart before he, too, slipped into a deep slumber.

CHAPTER THIRTEEN

Dublin's sleep was deep enough to initiate one of his dreams, another dream from his painful past.

* * *

Dublin was 11 years old, sitting at the kitchen table with his father, Anthony Pearson, silently wondering how it was possible that his father was there sitting across from him. Anthony was not upset with Dublin, nor was he even angry. He hadn't been drinking. Dublin just sat there, sitting straight up but in some sort of a stupor. It was just transitioning to summertime, and the temperatures outdoors as well as inside the house were steadily growing hotter. The heat was at times unbearable.

"Aren't you going to eat, boy?" Anthony Pearson gruffly asked his son. Although his words sounded sharp, he still didn't sound angry.

"Yes, sir," Dublin responded at once, picking up his fork as he snapped out of his daze that the sound of his father's harsh, gravelly voice had abruptly pulled him from.

Anthony grunted in response and nodded, seeing that Dublin had begun to pick at his dinner. "You be sure and clean up after we get done eating," Anthony ordered sternly, yet not necessarily unkindly. "And after that, you need to finish all your other chores before you go to bed. It's getting late. We sat down late to eat tonight."

No threats, no yelling. Dublin wondered what was going on with his father. Despite his nonviolence, despite his amiable disposition, Dublin was beginning to grow apprehensive. He was not accustomed to his father speaking to him in that tone. Still, Anthony was not being nurturing or acting interested in him, so that hurt him. This was all businesslike, his interactions with Dublin. But at least he wasn't yelling. Dublin supposed he ought to be grateful for that.

Dublin ate his rations for the evening. Although it was light, it was something. He was deep in thought throughout his meal. However, once he finished, he noticed that his father still sat at his place, looking directly past him, a blank stare on his rough, weathered face. Dublin frowned, wondering again what was going on with his father tonight. He was so glad for a respite from his anger and violence, and he felt surprisingly rather concerned for his father.

"Father, do you miss Mama?" he asked softly. His quiet voice reached Anthony's ears gently, and for a brief moment, Anthony's demeanor softened noticeably. But then the anger switched on, and he informed Dublin, rather spitefully, "I miss her every day of my miserable life. I've told you, and I'll tell you again 'til you understand. It should have been you and not her." He then cursed vehemently, taking the Lord's name in vain.

Anthony added, "Even if there was a God, He would have had mercy on me by now and taken you away, too. Then I'd finally be happy. I'd be rid of you and not have to look at you and be reminded of Destiny ever again. Your eyes are just like hers, and you act too much like her. Even so, you're helplessly and hopelessly weak and timid. I keep on mistakin' you for my daughter and not my son. You ain't ever gonna be good enough to amount to anything, not as a son of mine or anything worthwhile, not ever. You are completely worthless and a disappointing failure."

Dublin tried with all his might to hold back his tears. He was consumed with such pain that he didn't think he'd be able to bear it. Anthony's insults had hit him hard. His harsh words tore into his heart as with a newly sharpened sickle. Those words somehow hurt worse than all the beatings. He couldn't even feel the half-healed wounds he wore on his back from the other day.

He could feel the tears winning the fight. They slid down his perpetually bruised cheeks in fast-flowing streams. His blue eyes shone, but they were not alight with light or life. They were shiny with an ocean full of mournful tears from all the heartbreak and despair.

Dublin wept in utter brokenness, aware of all this pain that truly felt more ripping than he'd ever felt after the extended and sinister encounters he'd had with his whip-wielding father. He was dead inside. He was hopelessly hollow, unloved, and rejected.

"Just go to bed, Dublin," his father barked. "I ain't havin' this talk with you. I hate talking to you. You don't ever understand. You're too dull to learn anything I try to teach you. You are just too stupid. Useless! Get out of my sight. Now! Since you ain't able to stand what I have to say, which is the truth, you just get out of here, and quit bawling like a little baby while you're at it."

Ashamed and diminished to nearly nothing, Dublin bowed his head. A moment later, he boldly looked back up at his father who regarded him quietly now, looking to be tormented and as angry as he could be. Dublin's tears slowed, and he retorted loudly, disgusted, "If I'm so worthless and stupid, why do you bother keeping me around?"

Dublin typically would have been fearful of his father and how he might react after talking to him with such brass. But this time, he didn't care. Strangely, though, Anthony smiled at him. Dublin couldn't tell if it was sincere or just an attempt to disguise his father's true feelings toward him.

"Now that's my boy. That's my boy sayin' exactly what he thinks without reservation and saying it loud and clear instead of in a scared, little whisper or screaming in fear. And look! You've stopped crying. Now you're actin' like a man." His father sounded convincingly proud of Dublin. He waited several seconds, leaving Dublin in complete confusion.

Anthony's smile then quickly vanished, and his face became shadowed with a look of complete hatred and disdain for his puzzled son. Just as Dublin felt a newfound anticipation that his father was finally beginning to accept him—even if he didn't really love him—Anthony brutally vanquished any and all hope that Dublin might have felt regarding their strained relationship.

"But you're a day late and a dollar short, Dublin James. You and I both know you won't keep this newfound sense of confidence of yours. I know you all too well. You're nothin' but a rebellious boy and a sorry excuse of a son. I know once I have to punish you again, you'll run from me like a coward, and you'll scream like a frightened child, one much younger than you are. You're despicable. You ain't never gonna be good enough for me to love you.

"From the start you should have stood up for yourself and spoken up. I know if I would've done that, maybe my own father would've loved me. But I didn't. So he never loved me. Now you ain't gettin' loved, either. I won't do it. You don't deserve it. Just because Destiny saw good in you doesn't mean she was right. She could see good in any dumb fool.

"I only keep you around 'cause it's what your mother would have wanted. And just so you know, boy, I regret keeping her wishes every day. But," he said with staccato and a counterfeit smile that Dublin could see right through, a smile that though it was wide actually revealed his father's heinous heart toward him, "but just so you know, I'll never want you around. I hate you. I do."

Anthony's words were excruciatingly destructive yet spoken so calmly. In fact, they were spoken without much emotion at all. He was frighteningly calm but clearly full of shameless hatred.

Dublin was destroyed. He knew his life was never going to get any better and that he'd be better off dead—forever forgotten from his unstable father's memory. He was lonely and heartbroken in such a way that he would never heal. There was no way out for him.

* * *

Dublin suddenly awoke from his dream, trembling, with big, shiny tears in his eyes. He furiously swiped at them with the back of his hand as he sat up on the sofa. He felt frightened, and his pulse rapidly raced as his thoughts reflected on his dream, just another devastating recollection of his former life with Anthony Pearson.

He took a deep breath, and by lamplight, he saw that Andy was still snoozing soundly in his chair, unaffected by any noise Dublin might have made during his dream or upon waking up. Soon his heart rate returned to normal, but he couldn't help but continue mulling over all the words his biological father had said to him in his dream. Though Dublin was surprised that he'd not had a nightmare where Anthony had physically harmed him, he still was not in any way relieved.

Maybe I should be glad, but Anthony's words were far more damaging. I can still hear his voice saying them to me, not caring how badly he hurt me. Dublin was resentful toward Anthony, but as he sat up on the sofa in his home with his rightful father nearby, there was quietness rather than chaos. Right then, he decided he needed and wanted to truly forgive Anthony Pearson, if nothing else but to try to move on, to try not to hate that man any longer. It was too heavy a burden to carry.

"Help me, Lord," he whispered softly as tears slid down his cheeks. His heart broke like thousands of sharp shards of shattered glass. "I cannot do this on my own. I want to forgive Anthony, but I don't quite know how. I want to forgive him for myself and for my own growth, to be able to let go of all the pain he caused me when I was a child. Though he is dead, I no longer want the burden of my hatred for him weighing me down. I no longer want to feel this raging anger toward him. I no longer want to remember the countless wrongs he did against me.

"Lord, You have helped me accept that my biological father was a man who was treated badly by his own father. I always knew that, ever since my mother vaguely shared that information with me. But I never accepted that as a valid reason for his treatment of me. Help me feel compassion toward him rather than hatred. I still don't think I can love him because I cannot approve of his abusing me, nor can I forget it, but—I *am* beginning to feel sorry for him." Dublin paused for several moments, overwhelmed.

"I love You, Father God. Help me to think like Jesus. I remember those who beat Him nearly to the point of death, mocked him, humiliated Him without remorse, and then nailed Him to the cross. Scripture states that His response was for You, Lord God, to forgive them, for they knew not what they were doing. Jesus loved them, too.

"I...I believe that my biological father didn't know what he was doing to me. He hurt so badly and drank much more than he could handle. And he was not a man blessed with a stable mind. He wasn't well, and while he hurt me often and too often went too far, he must have done his best.

"It wasn't good enough, but I believe he tried and then perhaps just gave up and gave in to all the pressures and pain he surely felt his whole life. He was sick, just so sick. I'm so sorry I hated him for so long.

"Forgive me, Lord. Despite how evil he acted, Lord, I know You are merciful and loving. I pray that he made it to heaven and that he's found what—or who—he's needed all along. I hope he found Jesus so he was able to reunite with my mama, the love of his life while he walked this earth. I also hope he made it to heaven so I can see him again and embrace him finally, so he will be able to hug me and tell me he loves me, too. For deep down, I always loved him, even when I hated him. The hatred consumed me as time went by, and now I am feeling it slowly leave my heart. Praise be to You, Lord. And thank You, Lord, for changing and softening my heart, for molding me to become more like You. Thank You for teaching me of Your love and compassion. Forgive me, Father God, and it's in Jesus's name I pray. Amen."

Dublin suddenly felt an overwhelming sense of peace flood into any remaining barriers within his heart. As he lay upon the sofa, he relaxed and fell asleep once again, exhausted yet content.

Chapter Fourteen

Andy opened his eyes after several moments had passed following Dublin's quiet, lengthy, audible prayer. He'd awakened toward the beginning of his son's heartfelt conversation with the Lord. He'd heard most of it, and his own heart warmed, full of admiration for the nearly grown young man.

Silently, Andy praised God for Dublin's ever-continuous spiritual growth. Tears gathered in his eyes, slowly trailing down his shaven cheeks as he observed the teenager sleeping peacefully, sprawled out on the sofa.

Andy's heart was glad, completely joyous that Dublin wanted to forgive his hardhearted father and that he realized his father had endured a difficult life as a child himself. He was joyous that his beloved son yearned at such a young age to love and to become more like Jesus, the Savior of the world.

Andy also carried deep feelings of resentment toward Anthony Pearson. But upon hearing Dublin's prayer, he realized something. Anthony was deceased, and he, too, ought to forgive the man for hurting the boy who'd miraculously become his own son. Nothing could change the fact that damage had been done to his boy, but Someone *could* change Dublin. The young man certainly had a willing heart and a humble spirit, and he was ever willing to be changed by God.

Taking a moment to allow feelings of satisfaction and gratitude to fill his heart to the brim, Andy continued to sit in his chair, reflecting on all his many blessings. Then he got up to fetch a glass of water. Afterward, he checked on his son who had gone back to sleep, and he smiled in complete satisfaction. His heart and life were full, indeed.

"Good night, my son," he whispered ever so lightly, running his right hand through Dublin's short, wavy hair. Dublin shifted in his sleep and then snuggled closer against the pillow on which his head lay.

Andy left his son to sleep on the sofa, not having the heart to disturb him since he was sleeping so peacefully. It was growing late enough for Andy to head to bed. He was certainly exhausted enough to retire to bed for the night. He climbed the stairs to his bedroom, ignoring the heavy feeling of pressure weighing in his chest somewhat painfully. Breathing hard by the time he made it all the way upstairs, he walked more slowly into his bedroom. He carefully climbed into his bed.

Offering a short prayer of thanksgiving to the Lord for his son, Andy finished thanking Him for the day, closing his prayer by lifting up Carter Fallon, asking that he might be able to overcome his struggles and somehow find a way to let up on his drinking. Andy fell asleep mere seconds after he said amen.

Andy and Dublin had been asleep for some time when they were drawn from their sleep. They both heard someone knocking loudly at the front door. Dublin was startled—completely unnerved, truthfully—for it was only about 4:00 in the morning. It was earlier than he and Andy were accustomed to rising on any given morning. It was still totally dark outside. *Who could it be?*

Dublin slowly slid off the sofa, fear prickling at his back before it crept into his heart that was pounding hard inside his chest. Reluctantly, he began walking toward the door, although he knew he was too scared to answer it. Another sharp rap at the door sounded loudly. Dublin felt some reassurance when he realized that Andy was making his way slowly down the stairs.

"Papa, I'm scared," he admitted quietly as Andy came up behind him, placing a large palm soothingly on Dublin's narrow right shoulder. Andy moved to stand protectively in front of Dublin. He whispered in his ear, "Just stay back. I'll see who is out there. I have my pistol. We're safe."

Andy kept his own feelings of apprehension private to spare Dublin from feeling even greater fear. Dublin nodded imperceptibly in the darkness, moving aside. He stood behind and off to one side of his father while Andy took a deep breath. With his hand over his gun, he opened the front door.

Bravely, Dublin peered around his father, and his dark blue eyes met the sight of a man standing on the porch holding a lantern. His heart beat rapidly while he struggled to identify the man.

Andy recognized him right away. "Well hello, Sheriff Walters. I am certainly quite surprised to see you at my doorstep this early in the morning. Is...is everything alright, Daniel?"

Sheriff Walters pursed his lips, avoiding Andy's question for a few seconds. "May I come in, Andy?" His tone was weighted down with solemnity.

"Sure, come right on in, Daniel," Andy replied, stepping aside so the sheriff could enter the farmhouse. Daniel Walters removed his hat as he walked inside, looking rather daunted by something.

"What's the matter, my friend?" Andy asked quietly. Hesitation was present in his deep voice. He wasn't certain he truly wanted to learn what was troubling the sheriff. Walters, his head bowed, moved to look Andy in the eye, regret and apprehension clouding his own eyes.

"I'm afraid I've got distressing news, Andy. Harvey Adamson has escaped from his jail cell. And he had help. I came into work extremely early this morning, about 3:00. I couldn't sleep. When I arrived, Adamson was gone. It appears someone broke in, took a hacksaw to the iron bars of Adamson's cell, and sawed clean through them in one area, enough so Adamson could get out. I don't have any evidence of who busted him out of his cell, but no matter who did it, I'm afraid nobody in this area is safe with Adamson loose.

"And I'm sorry to say that the two of you are especially in danger. Please, I'm asking you two to be very careful until we can find him and bring him back into custody. As soon as I finish up here, I'm going to look for him."

Andy absorbed the disheartening information in stride, on the outside anyway. But inside, he was in turmoil. He feared mainly for his son's welfare. Glancing toward Dublin, he saw that the teenager's face was contorted in fear—pure, desperate, uncontrolled fear.

"Well, we'll certainly be cautious, Daniel. Thank you, sir, for making your way over to our place to give us fair warning. I will be praying that Adamson is brought in soon before anyone is harmed. I'll keep my gun close by at all times until I hear of his capture. Thanks again, Sheriff. I'll pray for your strength and safety as well. May the Lord offer you His protection and peace during this time."

"Thank you, Andy," Sheriff Walters said, shaking his friend's hand as all three of them moved toward the door. "Stay safe. Hopefully, Lord willing, this will all resolve soon."

Dublin couldn't seem to suppress the overwhelming waves of fear. Relentlessly, they crashed over him, nearly drowning him emotionally as they ominously buffeted at him with no mercy and no hope of escape that he could see in sight.

"Thank you," Andy said, walking Daniel Walters to the door. The sheriff offered him a brief, halfhearted smile and then tipped his hat to Andy before he made his way outside. He mounted his horse and was soon out of sight. Andy closed the front door slowly in utter disbelief. He then slowly turned to face his son.

"Well, son, that was quite some news to receive. I don't even know what to say, much less *think* of this," Andy commented, looking at Dublin and lacking the knowledge of how to properly handle the situation.

Dublin merely shook his head, unable to verbalize his thoughts regarding the matter. He was scared witless. He feared for both of their lives.

"Papa, do you think Mr. Adamson is going to come here after us to kill us?" Dublin had finally asked the heartrending question that cut Andy to the core.

Andy could only pray silently.

My 17-year-old son shouldn't have to ask this question. He should feel safe in his own home. But the truth of the matter is that we are not safe. This is really happening. Oh, Lord God, please watch over us. Please give Dublin the peace he needs to endure this. Please give him strength and courage, and help me keep him safe from any and all harm.

Only You, Lord, are in control. Help me to rest under Your control, to accept Your will as mine, and to know that You know what is best for us. Help us remember that You will never leave us nor forsake us. In Jesus's name I pray. Amen.

A strange sensation of peacefulness filled Andy's heart. Pulling Dublin close in a warm, secure embrace, he hugged his son tightly. Dublin hugged his papa fiercely as well. He, too, strangely felt at peace about the situation. Praying silently, he placed his very life and his trust in the One, the only One, who had faithfully delivered him from all dangerous situations thus far. He hadn't any reason to doubt that God would see him through this time. He surely would.

Dublin held on to his father for another few moments when suddenly they were harshly interrupted by the unmistakable sound of horse hooves pounding against the hard ground. Full-fledged dread rose up in their chests at the same time as Andy and Dublin quickly separated from their embrace. Andy drew his pistol and then peered out a window, seeing nothing. Darkness surrounded them. The sun still wouldn't rise anytime soon.

Successfully hidden from sight and cloaked by the dark night, two men intruded on the Caldwell property and sat on their horses, undetected. They were silent for several moments, save for the occasional snorting of their horses beneath them.

Andy leaned down, whispering urgently into Dublin's right ear. "Son, go. You know as well as I do who is outside. Run and hide, and stay there. I will do my best to fend off Adamson and whoever is with him. No matter what, do *not* come out from your hiding spot. I cannot allow that man to harm you again. Please go now, and always remember that I love you."

Dublin stared at his father, wide-eyed. He was in such disbelief that any emotion was far from him except for fear. He was terribly afraid of Adamson who was now right outside their house. But losing Andy and then surviving was his worst fear. He responded in a hurried, hushed voice, "I love you, too, Papa." Then he obediently fled upstairs, tears streaming down his face. He decided to claim a hiding spot in his closet. He was unsure whether it was a wise hiding place, but he couldn't think of another location where he could likely go undetected for at least a while. Hopefully, Andy would be able to defend against an intrusion.

A strong, deep voice called out harshly from outside. "Andrew Caldwell! I *know* you are in there. Come outside!"

Flinching, Andy gripped his gun more tightly. His heart beat nearly out of control, and his chest tightened painfully. "What do you want with me, Harvey Adamson?" he demanded, remaining still.

"You know full well what I want, Caldwell. I want your life and your son's life. After what you both have put me through, I'd say putting a bullet into both of your heads is warranted. Now come out, or we're coming in."

> *Lord, please keep us safe*, Andy prayed silently. *If this situation grows lethal, I ask You to keep Dublin safe from harm. He is innocent in this, and he's so young. Please take me, not him. He has his entire life ahead of him to live, to live for You.*

After a few more threats from Adamson, Andy finally complied, stepping outside his home. He was dismayed to see who it was that accompanied the escaped criminal and who was also determined to seek revenge on him and Dublin. He stopped, his heart sinking with dread and disappointment.

CHAPTER FIFTEEN

Andy's gaze settled on a stone-faced Carter Fallon who sat upon his mare in stoic silence next to Harvey Adamson on his horse. Neither man carried a lantern, but the moonlight illuminated both well enough for Andy to recognize them. He was also able to see that they both wielded firearms.

"Carter Fallon," Andy said, hurt and betrayal in his voice. "Why have you gone and done this? Why did you break this man out of jail so the two of you could come here and threaten my son and me? I have done you no wrong."

Carter Fallon sneered, his demeanor unswayed by Andy's stance on the matter. "Andy Caldwell, after you and that boy of yours left my house yesterday, you made it clear that you weren't going to have anything to do with me unless I gave up my drinking. I decided then that your friendships were worthless. You clearly think you are better than me. You always have thought that way. I already know I will never be good enough for the likes of you, so I took it upon myself to seek revenge against you by helping my *true* friend here out of jail."

Harvey glanced over at his companion with contempt, hissing at him through clenched teeth. "Shut up, Fallon. He doesn't need an explanation; he doesn't deserve one. Quit your talking, and let's just take care of business. Now!"

Obediently, Carter Fallon immediately cocked his pistol, aiming it toward Andy's head. Resigned, Andy closed his eyes, placing his life into the hands of God. But inside, his heart beat rapid-fire in an uneven, uncontrollable cadence. He even found it physically painful. He also deeply hurt inside for his son who would be left behind, if Dublin even survived this deadly encounter.

Fallon began to put a light pressure on the trigger. But he found he simply couldn't squeeze it all the way. He hesitated, knowing somewhere from within that murdering Andy would be wrong. But Adamson, filled with an unquenchable, intense rage at Fallon's hesitation and at Andy Caldwell for having him thrown into jail, thwarting his initial plans, fired his weapon without hesitation as his heart was overtaken by hatred. The bullet became lodged in Andy's home, somehow miraculously missing his head only by a mere inch or so. It buried deep into the old siding of the farmhouse, and somehow, Andy eluded certain death—for the moment.

Dublin, safe and secure in his dark, nearly suffocating closet, felt a desperate cry rise in his throat. He drew in a ragged breath before he bravely emerged from his hiding spot. Running down the staircase and through the dark house, he tore open the front door just in time to witness an infuriated Adamson cursing gruffly. His angry and vulgar words were directed at a petrified Andy. Adamson quickly pointed his pistol toward Dublin's father.

Reacting before he could evaluate whether it was a good idea, Dublin uncharacteristically shoved his father off to the side with all his might before sprinting toward the two men. Regarding the teen curiously, Adamson lowered his handgun as Dublin rapidly approached him on foot.

Andy staggered twice before regaining his balance after his son mightily pushed him aside. All he could do was stare speechlessly, incapable of moving. He knew he ought to do something, but not only did he not know what to do but he couldn't seem to break free from his current paralysis from fright, an overwhelming fright that governed his body regardless of what he willed it to do.

"Dublin, son, what are you doing?"

Dublin mustered all the strength he had, springing deftly from the ground before shoving the broad man directly off his tall, stout horse. All

Dublin knew was that he must act in order to save his father's precious life and hopefully his own, too.

Adamson toppled off his draft crossbreed, falling down by the horse's side opposite where Dublin had jumped him. The horse pranced nervously as Dublin tussled with the giant man. He somehow had remarkable strength considering his lesser size and milder temperament.

Finally, Dublin was able to wrestle Adamson's firearm away from his tight grasp. Then he held it against Adamson's temple. This was the first time he'd ever fought back in a situation where he or someone he loved was being threatened. And while it felt almost gloriously satisfying to hold the gun to Adamson's head, Dublin didn't have it in him to kill this man. Regardless of Adamson's ruthless attempts to kill him and his papa, Dublin just couldn't do it.

Finally able to move but still somewhat stunned, Andy began making his way to his son and Harvey Adamson. He noted that Dublin still held the gun shakily to the criminal's head. He was glad his son was able to muster the bravery to take extreme measures to keep them both safe, but he was also immensely regretful that Dublin had been forced to step out of his typically kind demeanor and do something he never would have dreamed of doing. But Andy need not worry about these things at this very moment.

Right now, he knew he ought to step in and try to take control of the situation before it grew catastrophic. Dublin handed Harvey's pistol to Andy with relief. While it had felt nice to be capable of doing something to protect his father and himself, he truthfully hadn't enjoyed holding the bad man's life in his hands.

Harvey Adamson regarded Andy as he took the gun from his son. He believed that Andy would have enough resentment toward him to shoot him, so he lurched at Andy without hesitation in a desperate attempt to disarm him.

Seeing no other option, Andy reluctantly but forcefully raised his right arm high and then brought the pistol down hard on Adamson's head, effectively knocking the dangerous man unconscious.

Carter Fallon was watching the situation unfold in silence. Deep down inside his own hurting heart, he felt remorse for Andy Caldwell whom he had claimed as his friend until yesterday's events occurred, causing a great sense of doubt and coldness to well up in him. And he knew that he was to blame.

Fallon knew he had a problem, if not many problems, and now he'd clearly crossed the line. He'd burned it as well, for surely Andy would never offer him forgiveness for nearly taking his life and Dublin's, regardless of whether he actually would be forgiven or forever despised and rejected. Carter dismounted his Appaloosa mare and made his way quietly over to Andy, kneeling beside the crumpled, unconscious man and toward Dublin who was standing wide-eyed and wary as he approached them.

Without speaking, Carter Fallon produced some rope from his jacket pocket. Binding Adamson's wrists, he found the act reminiscent of tying up that man once before and for similar reasons. Intense guilt wracked his soul, and after he completed his task, he made eye contact with Andy. He was nearly altogether rattled by Andy's expression that was visible to him by way of the milky moonlight.

This man who Carter and Harvey almost violently robbed of his life just looked back at Carter with compassion and forgiveness in his warm, expressive, dark eyes. Andy reached out his right arm slowly, an unexplained smile in his eyes, offering his hand to Carter Fallon. Fallon recoiled slightly, not understanding how Andy Caldwell could even fathom forgiveness and friendship following the events that had just unfolded moments ago.

"Andy," Fallon said, his voice cracking and revealing all the brokenness and heartache within him. "I do not deserve to be your friend. You don't have to pretend like everything is alright, like none of this ever happened just now. I am a pathetic excuse of a man and a pitiful friend. I deserve to die a miserable death, and there's no remedy for how I feel or for what I have done against you and Dublin. You both were the only two friends who have ever truly cared, who ever accepted me for who I am. I am worthless. Please, this cannot be overlooked. I'll understand if you take my pistol and shoot me. In fact, I beg you to do it, or I will do it myself."

Immediately, Andy reached out, placing his hand gently on Carter's left shoulder. The broken man pulled away, loathing Andy's kindness and acceptance, scrambling for his gun before Andy could even offer a word of encouragement or hope.

Andy could see that Carter was in desperate need of God's saving grace now more than ever before. But Carter was already bringing his gun to his head. Andy paused briefly, asking for guidance from the Holy Spirit in blind faith.

Dublin watched his former teacher move to end his life in an eerily similar manner as he had attempted as a young boy when his life had seemed hopeless. It was when all he thought he knew had become an unattainable mystery.

He recalled that the only father who had ever loved him could die today or live only to be severely handicapped, while the man who had given him life but who had never loved him was dead. His biological father's last words had implored Dublin to forgive him, and those last words still made him feel unloved.

Dublin knew he had to act before it was too late. Mr. Fallon still stood there, a heartbreaking expression on his face betraying the man's hopelessness and crippling pain. He still held the gun to his head.

"Mr. Fallon, will you please hand me your gun?" Dublin asked, emotion overtaking his deepening voice. "Please. I'd like to talk with you. I want you to know that you are not alone."

Dublin held his hand out slowly to Carter Fallon who complied with some reluctance. Carter handed Dublin the gun, who passed the firearm to Andy who promptly unloaded it and tossed it aside, out of reach. Andy was pleased with Dublin's reaction to this situation that had to be traumatizing for the teenager. But by God's grace, he was strong enough to reach out to this man, this man who had now clearly reached the ultimate breaking point in his life.

Andy continued to keep his heart prayerfully attuned to the Holy Spirit while he observed his son's efforts to share the hope of the gospel with Carter Fallon who had been blind and deaf to the Word.

Andy prayed silently, *God, maybe You will use Dublin and speak through him to enter into this man's hardened heart, this man who is overcome by pervasive, long-lasting hurt. Please, Lord, do this for him.*

"Mr. Fallon," Dublin spoke. "First I would like to share with you that I almost ended my life, too, and in the same manner. I nearly shot myself with my papa's gun. The only reason I am still standing here today is because the gun turned out to be empty. But I believe—more than that, *I know*—that God saved me, my life, *and* my soul through the shed blood and the sacrifice of His Son, Jesus. I was at the lowest point in my entire life. All my hopes and dreams and reasons for living had been violently taken from me. I was helpless, and all seemed hopeless.

"But something—or rather Someone—came to my rescue, and I cried out to the Lord Jesus, confessing my sins and my need for Him as my Savior. I asked for forgiveness, and I'm not kidding you, the burdens in my heart that weighed me down physically on my shoulders were instantly lifted. I felt a noticeable sense of unexplained and unexpected peace settle over me, as well as an incredible joy because of the knowledge that through Christ Jesus, God saved me and loves me so, so very much.

"Mr. Fallon, you can have freedom and eternal life in Jesus, too, and everything else that you need. Only He can make any one of us whole, and His joy is above anything that gives us joy in this world. He can forgive you and save you, giving you hope that will withstand all and a permanent home in heaven with God our Father. And then, the Holy Spirit will indwell your heart, forever acting as your guide and leading you toward what is righteous. All you have to do is ask Him. Would you like for me or my papa to pray with you?"

Andy was astonished by Dublin's eloquence and bravery. He silently praised God, thanking Him for speaking through his precious son so wisely. He waited for Carter's response to Dublin's God-led words.

Carter Fallon hung his head, looking defeated and utterly broken, but he wouldn't respond. Instead, he sank slowly but decisively to his knees. As Fallon knelt on the cold, hard ground, Andy and Dublin observed him with his head still bowed. He wept quietly. They both recognized that Fallon was going through something devastating, but they held on to the hope that he was silently praying to God, saying a life-changing prayer, a prayer that would allow the Lord's mercy and grace to prevail and allow salvation to be granted to their deeply troubled, broken friend.

Andy and Dublin simultaneously prayed silently on Carter's behalf. Even though the man spoke not a word aloud, they could tell he was reaching toward God. His humble stance and his flowing tears were a good indication.

Finally, Carter's weeping ceased. He choked back a violent sob and looked up from where he knelt, making eye contact with first Andy and then Dublin. And then he smiled, a smile filled with joy and victory. Tears were still shining in his gray eyes, and neither father nor son could dispute the sudden, miraculous brightness that filled those eyes or the confidence and peace that now seemed to reside within the transformed man.

Carter slowly stood up and then immediately embraced Dublin. He expressed genuine thanks to the boy for taking the time to lovingly share what he needed to do in order to receive salvation. Dublin felt tears gather in his sapphire eyes. Earnestly, he returned his friend's hug, his friend who was now unquestionably a brother in Christ. Then he turned to Andy who was watching him, awestruck and moved, unable to speak. Carter tentatively moved to give his friend a hug when Andy finally offered him his classic, authentic smile full of warmth right before embracing him in a hearty hug.

"Andy…" Carter began, his voice momentarily trailing off. "Andy, I just, I am so sorry for all I put you through. Though you were undeserving, and I knew it, I was embittered. I betrayed you. I endangered your life, along with Dublin's. Though I know the Lord has forgiven me and that I am right with God and that Jesus has saved me, I do hope you'll forgive me.

"I desire to be your friend for always, and I hope you and Dublin truthfully want the same. I am forever indebted to your love and loyalty. The fact that you two cared enough to help me come to know Christ and not just let me die by my own hands, I…I can never repay your generosity and concern. Thank you, and I hope you gentlemen know that I love and appreciate you. I deeply value your friendships."

Andy smiled broadly, the joy spreading across his entire face. "Well, we love you, too. All is forgiven, and our friendships aren't threatened in any way. Right, Dublin? God is certainly good, and He is going to see to it that we continue to bond, that we are going to be brothers in Christ forever. I want you to know that I can help you if you have any questions about the Bible or about our God. We can hold Bible studies together so you and Dublin and I can continue to grow."

Carter smiled, saying in a soft tone, "Thank you, both of you. I'd like that very much." He paused for a moment, relishing the newfound sensations and wonder of this peace and joy he felt and the relief from his burdens of sin and despair that had once seemed unceasing and relentless but that were now lifted by a freely given gift of grace.

Carter spoke again, this time on an entirely different matter, sounding spooked. "Oh, what are we going to do about Adamson? He's likely going to come to in a matter of moments. We probably ought to try to haul him back to the jail and see if Sheriff Walters can see to it that he's locked up securely."

"Yes, most definitely," Andy agreed. "Carter, can you help me sling him over his horse?" Andy glanced over at his friend.

Carter nodded affirmatively, and he and Andy worked together to lift the broad, unconscious man up and over his big horse. Harvey Adamson moaned incomprehensibly as he was slung across his mount, facedown. By all appearances, he was still knocked out cold.

Andy and Dublin rushed toward the barn to tack up their horses. Carter mounted his horse, leading Harvey by his horse's bridle. He reined his horse toward the barn to wait until Andy and Dublin came outside with their mounts.

Andy worked quickly alongside his son, and before long, they both had their horses tacked up and ready for a trip into town. In the moonlight, Andy glanced over at his beloved son, both sharing a joyful smile. They felt content trusting that the Lord would work out everything in their favor. And now surely He would also work things out for their friend.

CHAPTER SIXTEEN

The year 1882 began and brought with it an abundance of good times and cheerful hearts for Andy, Dublin, and Carter Fallon. Although Carter lost his property to foreclosure shortly after Harvey Adamson was jailed for the second time, Andy warmly welcomed his friend into his home to live peaceably with him and his ever-maturing son for as long as he needed to.

Carter was diligent, helping with the upkeep of Andy and Dublin's home. He also helped care for Andy's horses whenever Andy needed a break from the grueling, daily physical work. Carter had to admit that he enjoyed the rewarding work, the feeling of being needed and appreciated, and the reassuring state of belonging that he now felt as sort of an adopted addition to the Caldwell family.

Andy was deemed as healthy as possible by Dr. Nicholas at every scheduled appointment, but he still suffered sporadic days where his heart failure limited his ability to work and do leisurely activities.

Still, he persevered and continued to take the foxglove extract religiously. Perhaps even more importantly, he faithfully placed his life into God's loving hands every day when he woke up.

Dublin continued to grow in leaps and bounds. Even though he was well aware of his need for continuing spiritual growth, he felt confident in how far he'd come since the days of being a lonely, abused, unwanted boy. The Lord would continue to place only goodness within him.

God would renew Dublin's mind, heart, and soul with an everlasting faithfulness, never leaving him empty or forgotten. Dublin already had experienced many monumental changes in his life that, to him, were undeniable proof of God's love and His grace and mercy. He was amazed by the rich blessings that God abundantly poured over him, granting him a hope that would always endure no matter the circumstance or any changes he might experience as he entered adulthood. Though he was not rid of pain and all the downfalls of living in a fallen world, he was being made whole and renewed each day. He'd been blessed so greatly to have been an instrument in Carter's salvation. It was something Dublin never could have foreseen, especially after experiencing that difficult day when Mr. Carter Fallon, as his oppressive school teacher, had mocked and threatened him.

All glory and honor goes to God, Dublin prayed. *No one but He alone can save. And even though Mr. Fallon, in my worldly opinion, was one of the least likely recipients of God's grace, well, we all have strayed like sheep and followed our own ways.*

This was done for God's glory and for His great purposes. I'm so joyful for Mr. Fallon's new life in Christ and second chances. He has been a wonderful addition to our household. I am happy for the help he faithfully and kindly offers Papa.

Thank You, Father, for everything. I hope Mr. Fallon's story offers many others hope in You. I hope my story does, too, for the furthering of Your kingdom.

Even though Dublin felt a curious empathy for his twice-attempted murderer, Harvey Adamson, he'd been vastly relieved when he received news that the man had passed away in jail in the middle of March from apparently natural causes.

It was now May. No longer were Dublin and his father in danger of that man ever harming them again. Dublin was surprised that he was compassionate toward Adamson, but his ever-softening heart simply wouldn't allow him to harbor hate or resentment toward him, no matter the severity of Adamson's crimes.

Cruelty was not foreign to him or forgotten throughout his young life. Even so, kindness was now much more prevalent. Lavished upon him greatly were a love and a kindness not easily forgotten or forsaken since the Spirit of God had indwelt him, guiding him throughout his treacherous journey of life.

The Holy Spirit was continuously drawing him ever nearer to God the Father, transforming him, although he was an imperfect being, into a more Christlike being. While Dublin could not expect to attain perfection, his very life, his attitudes, his ability to choose love over hate or revenge, and his slowly fading trauma from his past were all unfolding right before his own eyes in a pleasing manner in his own way. That was proof that he would never remain the same as he was before he accepted the free gift of eternal life. That had turned out to be so much more than merely a ticket into heaven. So much more!

Hope endures. It's always there, never leaving, and it starts when a soul chooses life over death. For Jesus is life. He holds the power to save and change the coldest of souls, the vilest of offenders, and the most rebellious of humanity into a holy, righteous, humble person complete with the unlimited right to a deep and personal relationship with the Lord.

Dublin was glad he'd chosen rightly on the day of lost hope. That hope was ultimately restored in a desperate leap of faith. And he was grateful that he had a hopeful future with his papa as well as his dear friend he looked up to—his uncle Carter, as he now called him.

Thankfully, his past was becoming further and further away. Though it once had been a devastating reality, he, through God, was healing and was now more able to look ahead toward the future and not behind so often as he used to. His life was much more fulfilling and fruitful than he'd ever expected, and he would always hold tightly to the promises he'd been granted mercifully. He'd hold tightly to the hope that he would always be taught new things by the Lord in order to live life more abundantly. He was confident that he would someday move on from certain strongholds, things, and people who were powerless to ever harm him or sway him another day in his life.

Dublin stared out the window as an extravagant sunset brought the good day to a close. His papa was sitting in his chair, doubled over and laughing at a comical comment that Uncle Carter just made. Carter was also laughing brightly as he sat comfortably on the sofa.

Dublin turned to look at Andy and Carter, his true family. He smiled, moved by a familiar peace settling into his heart and enveloping him with a warm, welcome, healing sense of contentment.